THE CHANGELING CONSPIRACY

Also by Helen McCloy

THE CHANGELING CONSPIRACY

HELEN McCLOY

A Novel of Suspense

DODD, MEAD & COMPANY · NEW YORK

Library of Congress Cataloging in Publication Data

McCloy, Helen.
    The changeling conspiracy.

    I. Title.
PZ3.M13358Ci   [PS3525.A1587]   813'.5'2   76–25862
ISBN 0–396–07370–0

To Richard and Estelle Harvey with love

Contents

The characters in this story are all fictitious, but Potter's Alley, Jefferson Place and the Hotel Moxon are real. I have merely changed their names and disguised their neighborhoods.

PART ONE

Attack

Who rides so fast through night and storm?
It is a father with his child . . .
"Father, you see the Elf-king near?"
"Child, it's only a wreathe of mist . . ."
"Father, you hear the Elf-king's call?"
"Child, it's only the wind in the leaves . . ."

Goethe, *The Elf-king*

1

In his late sixties Adam Endicott was still nimble in mind and body.

That was why I noticed his hesitation now.

He didn't speak until we were settled with our drinks in wing chairs on either side of the living-room fireplace.

Even then he was at a loss for words.

"Sam . . ."

"Yes?"

"How old are you?"

Direct questions were not Adam's usual style either, but I answered just as directly: "Thirty-two."

He sighed. "That's what I thought. Do you know how old Kate is?"

"Not exactly."

"Eighteen."

I tried not to feel angry. A father who brings up a daughter who has no mother to share his concern is always defensive.

Adam had trouble going on. I did nothing to help him.

At last he said: "I've only known you two years, Sam. You don't talk much about yourself. Have you ever been married before?"

"No."

3

"When we first met you told me you had been a stringer for the *Washington Post* in Phan Rang. Why did you bury yourself alive on a small-town newspaper when you got back?"

"Perhaps I wanted to forget Vietnam."

"Why should you want to forget Vietnam?"

"Doesn't everybody?"

"I don't want to forget Hué. Of course I was there as an archaeologist, not as a soldier or a newspaper man and—"

I was saved by the sound of a car pulling into the kitchen driveway. Greenwood is more country than suburb. The Endicotts' place was an old farm with only a footpath to the front door.

In the kitchen Kate's Scottie barked once. I couldn't tell whether this was a joyous bark of recognition or a warning bark of suspicion. Robbie was the world's worst watch dog, who would welcome anyone who approached him amiably.

Could it be Kate herself he was greeting?

She was at the University of Connecticut now, with no car of her own, but there was usually a Greenwood boy on hand to drive her home for weekends and this was a Friday. That was one reason I had picked this day to talk to Adam. I wanted to talk to Kate, too.

A boy's voice said: "Hello, pooch!"

A girl's voice said, more gently: "Down, Robbie!"

Quick steps pattered down the passage and Kate came into the room.

Her mother had been Vietnamese. Her native name meant First Light. To me she always had the quiet freshness of the moment just before dawn.

The first time I saw her, two years ago, she had been in a crowd of robust, uninhibited American high school girls and I thought then: She is like a flower in a vegetable garden. Perhaps I had been in Asia too long.

The axis of her almond eyes was tilted, but she had missed

4

the epicanthic fold in the upper eyelid which Mongolians are said to have evolved as an adaptation to extreme cold. Her people had traveled far since that prehistoric time. The very word Vietnam means "people of the south." Her richly black hair and ivory skin looked tropical.

Adam had given her a Western education, and yet . . . Once or twice I had surprised in her eyes, on her lips, that look dear to Buddhist scholars, the "archaic smile." It is a blend of irony and compassion, each honed to its finest edge. You see it only in the older Buddhist sculpture.

This afternoon she was looking as Western and liberated as she really was in rumpled shirt, jeans and sneakers, but under the shirt collar was a gold chain so delicate it was almost invisible. Threaded on it was a single bead of carnelian minutely engraved with the Chinese characters for peace and longevity, the kind of thing Asiatic mothers and nurses have been putting around babies' necks for thousands of years. Kate always wore it no matter what else she was wearing.

She smiled at me as she kissed her father.

"Sam, you know Joey Alfieri, don't you?"

The boy had followed her into the room. He was one of two or three pimply youths who had been trailing around after Kate ever since she was sixteen. His pimples were gone now, but he still had the soft, unfinished face of a puppy.

She turned back to Adam. "Father, have you seen squatters in that old house in the woods down the road?"

She never called him "daddy." The Vietnamese have two traditions of formality, Chinese and French. Some children still drop their eyes in the presence of elders. Some parents still exact a *vous* from children they address as *tu*.

"How far down the road?" asked Adam.

"Three miles, at least. The roof's falling in and all the windows are broken."

"That's the old Delano place. It's been empty for years.

What makes you think there are squatters there now?"

"We didn't actually see any," said Joey. "But we heard them just now as we drove past."

I was watching Kate. "And you didn't like what you heard?"

"No." Her neat little profile was suddenly hard and precise as if it had been carved in chisel-resistant jade. Something had frightened her, but she seemed unable to communicate her fear to her father.

"What was it?" I asked her.

Footsteps on the front porch. A tap on one of the front windows. "Anybody home?"

It was Isolda Marriott, who lived in a high Victorian house, all sharp points and angles, across the road, the only other house near this one.

She had a way of dropping in whenever she saw Adam's car in the driveway. She was not a man-eater, just one of the "sentimentally unemployed." Her marriage had ended in divorce and her daughter, Clara, lived in New York. Isolda's laugh was just a little too hearty when she told us that the only mail she got these days was junk mail and bills.

"Why, Kate!" It was a "carrying" voice, one of those that project to every corner of a Zoning Board or PTA meeting without a microphone. "I had no idea you were here. Clara will be home tomorrow evening. Do call her. She misses you."

"And I miss her," said Kate. "She and I and Joey used to have such fun when we were all at school."

"You mean after school," said Joey. "It was never fun at school."

"But doesn't it seem like fun now we look back at it?"

"That's what old soldiers say about old wars. Don't let the past fool you."

Isolda was trying to make herself small on a hassock near the hearth. Her parents must have foreseen that she would grow up on generous lines when they named her Isolda, but, instead of making the most of her splendid height, she went through life in a permanent crouch trying to look like a sex kitten.

Adam brought her a drink. "Do you know if there are squatters at the old Delano place?"

"No, but I'm not surprised if there are," she answered him. "It should have been boarded up years ago."

"Who owns the place now?"

"Some bank probably. Do squatters worry you?"

"They worry Kate."

Isolda turned to her. "Why?"

"When Joey and I passed the house just now we heard a child crying. Who would take a child to live in a place like that?"

"Only people who were quite desperate," said Isolda.

"Or quite vicious," said Adam.

Joey looked at his watch and rose. "I have to be getting home now, Kate. Want me to stop at the Delano place and find out what's going on there?"

"I wonder if that's wise," said Adam. "There may be nothing to this but some young mother walking through the woods with a fretful baby."

"It didn't sound like that," said Kate.

Everyone was drifting towards the kitchen with Joey. It was his quickest route to the driveway where he had left his car. Only Kate and I fell behind the others.

She seized the chance to whisper: "How did it go?"

My arm slid around her waist of its own volition.

"Not too good. He's worried about my age and my past."

"Oh . . ." It was more sigh than exclamation.

"Give him time. He'll come round."

I was leaning down to kiss her when Joey came to the door of the kitchen passage. "Kate, where are you?"

Before he could take it all in, my arm had dropped from her waist and I was smiling down at her instead of kissing her.

7

"That was a practiced manoeuvre," she whispered. "Too practiced for a nice young man."

"I'm not young and I never said I was nice." I raised my voice. "What is it, Joey?"

"I just want to say goodbye to Kate and remind her we have a tennis date tomorrow."

In the kitchen the back door was open. Adam flipped a wall switch and the twilight beyond the screen door became black night. The kitchen itself was now a hollow cube of light, like a brilliant stage.

A low growl rumbled in Robbie's chest and exploded in one curt bark, the canine sentry's warning shot.

A car was pulling into the driveway. Glare from its headlights slashed across the unshaded windows as it turned and stopped.

"Who can that be?" Kate went to peer through the screen door.

I could just make out the dim figures of a man and a woman in the darkness beyond the fine mesh of the screen.

He mumbled something about an accident, then spoke a little more audibly.

"May we use your telephone?"

"Of course. Come right in." Kate unlatched the screen door and threw it open.

Now I could see that both of them wore stockings pulled down over their faces.

The man aimed a revolver at Kate.

The woman seized her by one arm and began to drag her across the threshold.

"Let me go!" cried Kate.

Rob Roy was only a little dog, but he went for the woman's ankles. She kicked him. She was wearing a man's thick-soled boots under her long, limp dress.

I launched myself across the room. I was out of practice. I

didn't get to the gun in time. A blast burned my cheek and a blow struck my forehead.

The last thing I heard was a cry from Kate: "Not me! Oh, please not me!"

2

I had never realized before that kindness can hurt. Everyone in the hospital was so unnaturally kind that I was constantly reminded of my reason for being there. That hurt.

To survive, I had to detach myself from past and future. Time would only be manageable if I could chop it up into moments and deal with each one separately as it came.

Fight off nausea and dizziness. Lie still when a dressing is changed. Open the mouth for pill or thermometer. Let go and slide into oblivion when a needle pricks.

It didn't work. I was haunted by unanswerable questions. Where was Kate? What was happening to her now?

After a while I began to suspect that the small detachment I had achieved was not voluntary. It was an effect of the pills and needles. I was losing control of my own mind and will.

This suspicion led to my first voluntary act since I had entered the hospital. When the little night nurse came with another pill early next morning as she went off duty, I took it meekly, but stored it in my cheek before swallowing the tepid tap water in the paper cup. As soon as she left the room, I spit it out into a piece of paper tissue and flushed it down the drain in the bathroom.

Oh, yes, I had a private bath. I was in what they call a

semiprivate room, two beds and one bath. The other bed was empty, made up with that sterile hospital precision which makes a bed look as if it never could be used for anything as human as sleeping or love-making.

Had Adam ordered this for me? Or was it standard hospital treatment in emergency cases if no other room was available? Or could it be that this privacy was really a form of detention in disguise with a policeman on guard outside the door to keep me from talking to other people? Were the police suspicious of me?

Now my mind was clear of drugs I could think about myself and Kate. I knew how much I loved her now. For her sake I had charged a man with a loaded gun.

I also knew that if I loved her considerately I would leave her alone. What had I to offer her? Nothing, not even myself. I had no self.

A doctor arrived a little after nine, a neurologist, who put me through the usual tests for head injuries, pricking various parts of my face with a sewing needle to make sure that my nerves were still working and testing the focus of my eyes.

"You were lucky."

I said: "Kate Endicott was not so lucky. Is there any news of her?"

"No." Sensibly he didn't try to offer sympathy.

"How long have I been here?"

"Only one night."

"Has there been a ransom demand?"

"It's too soon."

"How badly am I hurt?"

"A bullet-nicked bone at the temple, the thinnest part of the skull. A millimeter to the left and you wouldn't be here. Fortunately for you, it was not one of those cyanide bullets so fashionable among terrorists today, nor was it a dumdum. Your forehead was pistol-whipped. No fractures, according to X-

11

rays, and no nerve damage according to your responses just now, but you are still suffering from concussion and shock. You must lead a quiet life for some time to come."

"I have a living to earn."

"Your newspaper is giving you a month's vacation with pay. They would like an eyewitness story from you as soon as you're able to dictate it over the telephone. You'll have a scar on the right side of your forehead. If you don't want to bother with plastic surgery you can wear your hair a little longer and—Are you listening to me?"

"No. When can I get out of here?"

"Not for forty-eight hours at least and then—"

"Impossible. I want to be with Kate's father when the ransom demand comes."

He looked at me thoughtfully. I could almost see his mind balancing alternatives. Then he surprised me.

"I think I'll leave it to you. After all, you know more about how you feel than I do."

"That's an amazing admission for a doctor."

"I'm just being clever." He said it with a half-smile. "People born free rebel against coercion automatically, but give them responsibility and they think twice before they do anything foolish. Just keep in mind that, if you take on too much too soon, you'll be back here before you know it. There's a state policeman who wants to talk to you now. Feel up to it? He'll wait, if I say he must."

"I'd like to get it over with."

So that was how I first met Captain Carew.

He was in mufti that morning, but even then there was something paramilitary about his lean, hard body and erect bearing. His hair had been allowed to grow a little longer than regulations would have permitted a few years ago. This, like some other things about him, was a tacit admission that times were changing.

12

He, too, avoided sympathy, but he managed to create a feeling that the situation, though critical, was manageable and that all would come right in the end if I would just leave everything to him. A prisonside manner.

He had a tape recorder with him and carefully asked permission to use it. His first questions were perfunctory, or, rather, he thought they were perfunctory.

Name? Address? Occupation?

Samuel Rogers Joel. Beverly Road, West Greenwood, Connecticut. Newspaper reporter, *Greenwood News.*

Then he started to probe, delicately but persistently.

I knew this technique well. First, establish that questioning is a painless process. Then probe just a little deeper. Finally, take off your gloves, spit on your hands and go for the jugular.

"Have you any idea who the man and woman were?"

"No, they wore stocking masks."

"Was there anything about them that would help you to identify them if you saw them again?"

"Nothing I can recall."

"Professor Endicott says the first figure to come to the screen door was a woman wearing a man's heavy boots under a long dress. Could it conceivably have been a man wearing a woman's dress?"

"I suppose that's possible. She was tall and strong for a woman. I noticed that when she, or he, was struggling with Kate."

"What about the voice?"

"Hoarse, nasal, raucous. At the time I thought it the voice of a woman with a bad cold."

"But it could have been the voice of a man with a bad cold?"

"I suppose it could."

"Any other peculiarities? Dialect? Accent?"

"None that I noticed. She, or he, only spoke a few words."

"Has Miss Endicott any enemies?"

13

"Kate? Enemies?"

"I'll put it differently. Can you think of anyone she has injured however slightly?"

"Kate doesn't injure people."

"Injury can be subjective. You may be nice to everybody and still some kook will decide that you are out to get him."

"You're asking me if Kate knew anyone who was a closet paranoid. How can I tell?"

"Who were her closest friends?"

"Mostly young people she went to school with here in Greenfield. One of them was there last night, Joey Alfieri. They both go to Connecticut University. On weekends he often gives her a lift home in his car. Another is Clara Marriott, daughter of Isolda Marriott, who lives across the road from the Endicotts. Clara lives in New York now, where she has a job on some magazine, but she, too, comes home for weekends."

"Any other close friends?"

"None I've met. There's one I remember hearing about, Neil somebody. I can't recall his last name. I think he goes to Yale."

"What about domestic staff? Any old family retainers?"

"You're behind the times. Adam Endicott shares a professional, working housekeeper with two other households. She comes to the Endicotts a few hours every other day when the house is usually empty. You'll get no more from her than from the man who comes to read the meter."

"We're not getting much from anybody." Carew seemed to be thinking aloud, always a disarming ploy. "Miss Endicott's appearance ought to help us in tracing her. Eyes with the Mongol fold aren't easy to disguise."

"So you haven't seen her photographs yet."

"What do you mean?"

"Kate is only half Vietnamese. She doesn't happen to have the Mongol fold. With liquid powder, wigs and contact lenses,

14

the kidnappers could make her look like any race or mixture of races except Mongol or African. The only time they had to worry about her being recognized was the first few minutes after they drove away with her in their car."

"They didn't have to worry even then," said Carew. "They didn't put her in the car where she could be seen. They put her in the trunk. Mrs. Marriott saw them do it."

I thought of that cramped space, dark, hot, airless, claustrophobic. Then I tried not to think about it.

That was the moment Carew chose to go for the jugular.

"I need a little more background material, Mr. Joel. I'm told you were born in Pekin in 1944. Right?"

Everyone knows it's a mug's game to lie to the police. You are almost certain to be caught and then they throw the book at you. Unfortunately, I had no choice.

The only question was how to lie. Boldly or deviously? Whoppers or half-truths?

I had only a few seconds to decide, but you can do a lot of thinking in a few seconds. The basis of thinking, association, is measured in thousandths of a second. I've been told that nervous impulses travel from brain to tongue at a hundred miles a second.

I chose boldness.

"Want to see my passport?"

Not even a direct lie. I had not said I had been born in Pekin in 1944.

He smiled. I really think he believed me. Boldness usually pays.

"That won't be necessary," he said. "But I would like to know where you went to school and what you did in Indochina."

I told him I had gone to school in Shanghai while my father was American consul there and then to college at Middlebury in New Hampshire where they specialize in European languages, because my parents wanted to Westernize me.

"But you ended up in Vietnam?"

"In my senior year an editor of the *Washington Post* came to recruit people with a knowledge of French for work in Vietnam. He noticed me because I knew Cantonese as well as French. He thought I could pick up colloquial Vietnamese quickly if I were on the spot. He said it was a tone language, like Chinese, but easier to learn. Unlike Chinese, people speaking one dialect could understand most of the others and there had been a Romanized script since the seventeenth century, thanks to French missionaries. So he sent me out to Vietnam as a stringer."

"What's that?"

"The lowest man on the totem pole. I was responsible for one small territory. I had no byline. I was paid according to the amount of news I could dig up or invent. It's a beginner's job. After all, in 1966 I was only twenty-one."

"When did you leave?"

"In 1974."

"Adam Endicott was there from 1955 to 1968. So your stay and his overlapped by two years. Did you know him out there?"

"You're like Europeans who say: 'Oh, you live in New York? They you must know my cousin who lives in Texas!' The Endicotts were in Hué. My paper's head office was in Saigon. I was moved around quite a lot but I never got farther north than Phan Bong. I was an apprentice newspaper man. Adam was a distinguished archaeologist and Kate was eight or nine. We were most unlikely to meet, especially with the war making transportation difficult."

He looked at me as if he did not believe me. That was curious, for this part of my story was the one part that was unimpeachable. I had never seen either Kate or Adam until I arrived in Greenfield. I was reminded that the true and the plausible are rarely the same.

He tried another tack now. "Why were you exempt from the draft? College?"

"No. Rheumatic fever as a child. Army doctors wouldn't take a chance on my heart. If they did and something went wrong my care would cost the government money."

"Why did you come home in 1974?"

"I picked up some bug, probably a fungus. Western medicine couldn't identify it. The thing finally went away of its own accord."

Did he believe all of this? Or some of it? Or none of it?

He wasn't stupid. He knew that either the yarn was true, or it was a cover story built up so carefully, layer by layer, that every detail could be checked out in surviving official records. Obviously I would not dare to be so specific if there had never been any Sam Joel, but . . . was I Sam Joel?

I think he wanted to believe it, at that point, yet he did ask one more question, the very question Adam had asked me yesterday: Why had I buried myself alive on a small-town newspaper when I got back? What future was there in Greenwood for a man like me?

The police need simple, comfortable motives to cope with the bewildering variety and inconsistency of human behavior; motives that can be expressed in one archetypal word: greed, lust, ambition, jealousy, revenge. An archetype is close to a stereotype, a printer's word, and the French printer's word for it is cliché. So I gave Captain Carew a cliché answer: "Homesickness."

"You wanted to find the sort of home here that you had never had?"

I had not expected him to be so perceptive. Was that one reason I had chosen a small town? Had I had too much of the rootless, cosmopolitan life? Or was it just that I felt less conspicuous and therefore safer in a small town?

Carew switched off his tape recorder and rose.

17

"Have you any questions to ask me?"

That was rather subtle of him. We all love to talk about ourselves and he had let me see him shut off the tape recorder. What a temptation to unburden myself of anything I had been holding back. Confiding in anyone is a delightful emotional luxury, but I had been through too many interrogations to be caught like that.

"Is this going to be the new style of kidnapping?" I asked him. "Bursting into a home with a gun and seizing a victim under the eyes of family and friends?"

"I hope not," he answered. "But there are fashions in crime as in everything human. The Hearst kidnapping set off an epidemic, a thirty-five percent increase in kidnappings in 1974, and 1975 was even worse."

"How can these kidnappers expect to get enough money from a man like Adam who has nothing but his pay and his savings?"

"Kidnapping is no longer just a crime against the rich. To-day's young, reckless criminal, the kind who will mug an old woman for her Social Security check, will snatch anybody for ransom, rich, poor or in-between, so everybody's in danger. People smiled when one of them asked for a ransom of only seventy dollars, but that's no joke to a family that doesn't have seventy dollars."

"Do you think these people are after money or something political?"

"We can't even guess until we hear from them."

"Unless we hear from them," I corrected him.

"Oh, we'll hear."

Was he humoring me? The prisonside manner again?

He paused on his way to the door. "How much longer will you be here?"

"I'm going home today. Getting up and doing things makes it a little more bearable than just lying here."

"I can understand that. My own daughter is just eighteen."

I was beginning to like him.

Then he spoiled it.

"Oh, by the way . . ."

I was instantly on guard again. Nothing is ever "by the way" in an interrogation. If a question of any importance is left to the last, it's done for shock effect.

"What about Kate Endicott's mother?" he went on. "Do you know where she is?"

"I have always assumed she was dead."

"There's no record of her death. According to Professor Endicott himself, she left him in Hué when Kate was only six years old. Later, there was a divorce in Paris. The last he heard of her she was married to a Frenchman, Ghislain de Boisron, but he has no idea where she is now."

And I had thought I was the only one with a secret.

3

The cheapest way to live in the country is to get a job as caretaker. Instead of paying the owner of the place rent he pays you a salary. Young people call this "house-sitting."

Our neighborhood between Greenwood and Eastport attracted big landowners who needed caretakers. They liked the distance from New York because it was just far enough to discourage a crowd of daily commuters. They liked the landscape of ponds and brooks and water meadows because the Eastport hydraulic company that owned most of it had to keep out factories and slums to avoid polluting the Eastport water supply—a kind of invisible zoning. They liked the few working farms because they provided fresh milk and eggs, and they liked the few really old houses, like Adam's, because they added historical interest.

One of the biggest of these landowners was spending a year in Morocco and I had been living in his gatehouse as caretaker since October.

My house was a little brick box, parlor, bedroom, kitchen and bath, built for a childless couple or a single man. There was mail-order furniture and dime-store crockery, sure to self-destruct in a few years. I had nothing personal to bring with me, so it was a house without past or future, about as homelike as a room in a motel.

Two things made my life there bearable: I had the run of the library in the big house and I had privacy. From my small stone terrace I could not see another dwelling, only the gardens of the big house and the trees beyond.

The terrace was the first place I went when I got back. I had already dictated my eyewitness story to a rewrite man over the telephone, making it as impersonal as I could. I had stopped to see Adam on my way home and he had promised to call me as soon as there was any news. Now there was nothing to do but wait for his call. I didn't want food or drink and I had given up smoking.

From the terrace I could see a faraway vista that looked like a dream of flower-scented lawns, empty in the evening light, silent except for birdsong. That was where Kate and I had gone when we first wanted to be alone together, only a few short weeks ago.

Ever since Eden gardens have been made for love. There we relive our oldest rituals. "The time of the singing of birds is come . . . our bed is green . . . thou hast doves' eyes . . . the joints of thy thighs are like jewels, the work of the hands of a cunning workman . . . how much better is thy love than wine . . ."

The telephone rang.

It was Adam.

"Can you come now? I need you."

It was dark when I got there. No police cars in sight. The police must be leaving a way open for the kidnappers to communicate with Adam, but there might be other, invisible watchers, the kidnappers themselves.

Adam met me at the kitchen door. Isolda was in the living-room and it was she who spoke first.

"Sam, I made him call you. Please find some way to keep him from doing what he wants to do now."

Adam sighed. "I only called you because I thought you might make Isolda see reason."

21

This could mean only one thing. "So you've heard from them?"

"Yes, they telephoned two hours ago."

"You said you'd call me the moment you heard. Remember?"

"I know, but I had second thoughts. I don't want to involve you or anyone else in anything so risky."

"I see. You've promised the kidnappers to meet them without telling the police. Isolda wants you to break your promise and tell the police so they can protect you."

"Exactly."

"How do you know it was the kidnappers who telephoned? Are you sure it wasn't some crank or crook cashing in on a newspaper sensation?"

"Quite sure. Would you like to hear the tape?"

"Tape?"

"The police said I should record all telephone calls. They left a tape recorder and a dozen tapes with me."

"Then the police are going to find out you're in touch with the criminals as soon as they play back their tape."

"No." Adam almost smiled. "When they come back I shall have substituted a tape of my own for this one, a blank to make up the right number."

"Are you sure the police did not leave a tap on your telephone?"

"They said they didn't. I'll have to take a chance they were telling the truth."

"Why not tell the police everything and trust to their experience in dealing with crooks?"

"That's what I say!" cried Isolda.

Adam shook his head. "These people aren't ordinary, down-to-earth crooks or gangsters. They are Walter Mittys with guns, daydreamers acting out in public their private delusions of grandeur. That makes them utterly unpredictable and infinitely dangerous. You'd better hear the tape. You'll never understand otherwise."

The tape recorder was on a taboret beside Adam's chair. He leaned over it to adjust the controls.

"Must you play it again?" said Isolda. "I don't think I can bear it."

Adam looked at her remotely. "Are you afraid Sam will agree with me when he hears Kate's voice?"

That jarred me. "Kate's . . . voice?" I faltered.

He flicked a switch. The spools began to spin slowly, silently, then a man's voice, deep as the hum note of a bass bell. A man with a big chest.

His speech was sloppy, deflated vowels, blurred consonants. Individual sounds were fused in an insect whine that rose and fell with a singsong beat that had nothing to do with meaning. I had heard numb voices like that before among the alienated, the drifting, the lost.

What slang there was seemed slightly out of date as if he were in late middle-age.

"You there, Adam Endicott?"

"Speaking." I could not wonder at the tremor in Adam's voice.

"You want your daughter back?"

"As soon as possible. Is she all right?"

"She is now." Pause for effect. "You want to keep her that way you better step lively. No fooling around with fuzz. Understand?"

"Yes."

"You got to swear. Say after me: I swear I won't tell the police or the FBI."

Adam repeated the words. I marvelled at the other man's naïveté. By his act of kidnapping, he had put himself outside civilization as well as law, yet he still saw his victim as someone bound by oaths and words of honor.

23

Was this a last echo of primordial magic? Your tribal god-demons will strike your enemy dead if he breaks an oath you force him to make in their names?

"What is it you want?" said Adam's voice on the tape. "Money?"

"Sure thing, but not for me. For the TFNH, the Task Force of the New Hashashin. I have taken the name of our ancient Master, Hassan-ben-Sabah, Sheikh al Jebal, and I shall strike as he struck, nine hundred years ago, without mercy in order to free the oppressed of the world.

"We are fighting for the disfranchised and the disinherited, the defeated and the neglected, the old, the sick, the children, and the jobless, the people who have no food, no medicine, no hope. For thousands of years, they have been ground to dust in every generation. Now we are going to feed them and clothe them, house them and cherish them and lead them back out of the darkness into the sunshine."

The words were not remarkable. They had all been said before. But the voice was remarkable. It had something no school of public speaking can ever teach, an intensity of feeling that would strike emotional resonance from any crowd. In speaking to crowds, as in singing, words don't matter. What matters is the rhythmic chant of the shaman's voice, powerful as the high note that shatters crystal.

Even I, a bitterly hostile and skeptical witness, forgot for a moment everything but the mass starvation I had seen in Asia.

And then he spoiled it.

His voice was suddenly no longer the voice of the prophet calling down the wrath of God on the ungodly. It was just the voice of a salesman trying to make a buck.

"To do this we need money. Lots of money. And we need it right away. We need a hundred grand, and if you want your daughter back, you'll have to get it for us.

"And don't you think of this as a kidnapping. Think of it

24

as war. Yesterday I issued a warrant for the arrest of your daughter, Katherine Endicott, in the name of the Task Force of the New Hashashin. We now hold her as a hostage for your good behavior. As a prisoner of war she will be treated with every consideration as long as you comply with our commands. If you don't, she will be executed. So you better get that money fast."

"I'll do everything I can to get it," said Adam. "But I don't think you quite understand my situation. I am not a rich man. I am a professor of archaeology and—"

"Don't give me that! Your kind is always making a poor mouth. I bet you got plenty. You just don't like to part with it."

"I don't have that much in cash."

"Then get it. Quick. From where I sit, a man is rich if he's got twenty bucks, but you don't know anything about that kind of poverty, do you? You think a man's poor if he doesn't get a new Rolls Royce every year, so you think you're poor. Quit stalling and get that bread. I don't care how you get it. Just get it. And have it by tomorrow night."

"Tomorrow night!"

"Why not?"

"Tomorrow's Sunday. The banks will be closed and—"

"So what? We want it in one hundred bills of a thousand dollars each. They'll all fit in one medium-sized manila envelope."

"Where am I to meet you?"

"Oh, no! You don't catch me that way. Telling you ahead of time so you can tell the cops. You just be ready to leave the house tomorrow evening any time after six. I'll call and tell you when and where to go when I feel like it. And you better be alone. Understand? Your daughter's the one who'll get it if you're not."

"How do I find my daughter?"

"We'll tell you that when we've counted the money."

"What if I can't get so much cash at such short notice?"

"You'll get it."

"But how can I be sure you really have Kate?"

"We thought you'd bring that up. Keep listening."

The resonant voice died away. I heard the almost inaudible whir of spinning reels again. Then came a scuffling sound and another voice, frail and breathy.

"Father . . . I'm all right . . . I'm kept blindfolded and my hands are tied most of the time, but I'm not gagged and you can tell I'm not crying . . .

"No one can possibly find me where I am now. I'll never get out of here unless you do as they say. So please do whatever they say . . . if you can . . . please . . ."

"I don't believe it!" cried Isolda. "That can't be Kate."

"It's her voice," said Adam. "I would know it anywhere any time."

I was as sure as he. Apparently Isolda couldn't face a thing like this. She had to pretend it wasn't there.

I had thought the tape was finished, but suddenly there came a woman's voice, hoarse as if her throat were clogged with mucous. The man's tone had varied from solemn to mocking. The woman struck only one note—malice. Her voice shook with it as she read a headline from the evening paper.

"Terrorists struck in the streets of Cairo yesterday. Three girls were killed by bombs."

That was all. That was enough.

I got up and walked around the room. I have never found it easy to sit still under tension.

Isolda spoke in a whisper. "What's to keep them from killing her once they get the money?"

"Nothing," said Adam. "That's one way to keep her from identifying them afterward."

"Then go to the police now!" Isolda was on her feet.

"No," said Adam. "I cannot take that chance."

"Is there a chance any other way?"

"That's the only chance there is."

She sank back in her chair. "They wouldn't know whether you'd been to the police or not."

I was amazed at her stupidity. "Oh, yes, they would. They'll watch him all the time now. They may even have a tap on his telephone. Adam, will you let me follow you in a car tomorrow night? A rented car they can't recognize?"

"Only a trained detective could get away with that. They'd spot you, Sam."

"And that would be really dangerous," added Isolda.

"How about my going in your place?"

"They're expecting me and they probably know what I look like now. This is like defusing a bomb. One mistake, however slight, can destroy us all at any moment."

"Perhaps you ought to warn the police to keep away tomorrow evening," said Isolda.

"I've already asked them to keep away until I need them," said Adam.

"You think they will?" I asked him.

"I hope they will," he answered.

"What about money?" said Isolda. "How are you going to raise a hundred thousand in cash before tomorrow night?"

"I shall try to get hold of the president of my bank tonight. I'm pretty sure I can get twenty thousand as a personal loan against my ninety-day-notice savings account, and I can probably get ten thousand more by taking a second mortgage on this house."

"And the seventy?"

"Loan sharks, I suppose. Won't they lend big amounts if the interest is high enough?"

"Don't be silly!" snapped Isolda. "I can let you have twenty by borrowing on my Treasury Bills, but you'll have to think of some way to beg, borrow or steal the rest."

I heard my own voice saying calmly: "I can get you another fifty in New York tomorrow."

Adam looked at me sharply. "You're quite sure you can manage a sum as large as that?"

"Quite sure."

He sighed. "An ordinary thank-you hardly seems adequate."

"Then don't say it," advised Isolda. "You know Sam and I want to do this or we wouldn't be doing it."

"I'll never forget you're doing it," said Adam.

I walked out to my car, thinking about the warning from the man who had given me that fifty thousand.

"Don't spend this all at once until ten years have passed. If you do, you'll be taking your life in your hands."

That was only two years ago.

4

Sunday morning one of the vice-presidents of my bank met me by appointment in their Fifth Avenue office. To obtain this favor I had had to tell him why it was necessary for me to get into the bank Sunday morning.

I thought it safe to do so for this is an old-fashioned bank that has been keeping the secrets of New York families for many generations, many of them more scandalous secrets than a mere kidnapping.

I needed his key as well as mine to open my safe deposit box so I could take out fifty thousand in Treasury Bonds which he proceeded to cash for me.

As a rule, I carry nothing but checkbook, credit cards and small change in my pockets, so I found it an ordeal to walk out of the bank with fifty thousand dollars in cash stowed away in an envelope in my breast pocket. It was a snug fit, but not bulky enough to make a bulge when I left my jacket unbuttoned.

I kept telling myself that I did not look like a man who would walk around with that much cash. I hoped that any muggers who happened to be in the neighborhood would agree with me. It is astonishing what you can get away with so long as you do not look the part you are playing.

I had only a short way to walk. I felt better the moment I

got into my car at the Hippodrome Garage and locked myself inside. I pushed firmly out of my mind all the movies I had ever seen about men being followed from banks and their cars forced off the road, but I was not really comfortable until I turned the money over to Adam in his own house.

One thing I found rather touching about that moment. He didn't count the money. This was a reflex left over from childhood training. His generation was taught to trust the honor of friends.

Isolda looked at me grimly.

"We're in trouble," she announced. "Adam's bank gave him the personal loan, but they won't give him a second mortgage. They say the house isn't worth that much. So we're short ten thousand."

I turned back to Adam. "Did you tell your banker what you wanted the money for?"

"Not precisely. I just said it was an emergency."

"Then you'll have to tell him now. It's the only way to get the ten thousand."

"That's what I've been saying!" cried Isolda. "Oh, why didn't you tell him this morning when you had the chance?"

"I promised I wouldn't tell anyone," said Adam. "It's bad enough to have told you and Clara whom I know and trust. If I start telling strangers . . ."

"The Hashashin will never find out you broke your promise," I told him. "How can they learn anything about a private conversation between you and your banker? But they will know in a few hours if you can't pay them the money they're demanding. That's the real risk to you and to Kate. How long will it take you to get back to that banker?"

"He's on the golf course now. I'd better allow thirty minutes to get there and at least forty to go back to the bank with him, plus another thirty to get back here. It's just four now. I should be back about twenty minutes of six."

"That's cutting it fine."

"I know. The Hashashin said they would call me any time after six. If weekend traffic is heavy, I might not make it."

"All the more reason for getting started at once," said Isolda. "I'll drive you, so you won't have to waste time looking for a place to park. Sam, do you think you can stall these people if they call before we get back?"

"I'll try."

So I was left alone.

I went into the kitchen and made myself a pot of coffee only to find I didn't want it.

Perhaps I was distracted by the place in the wall where the bullet that grazed my forehead had left a scar.

I knew a drink wouldn't do me any good. When you're in a state of "anxiety alert" you metabolize alcohol so rapidly it has no time to relax you.

When anxiety lasts for days or weeks, it cuts your personality in half. There is the true self, aware, exalted, dutiful, heroic, but there is also that other, baser self that eats, drinks and sleeps no matter what happens. The true self would like to dissociate its being from such gross, vegetable self-absorption, yet, without that vegetable self, the true self could not survive.

I was beginning to approach that divided state now. By tomorrow I would probably feel hungry again and even laugh if something absurd happened, but all the time, under the surface, the true self would be living in silent anguish and—

The telephone rang.

I looked at my watch. Ten after six.

"Hello?" I didn't identify myself. I just said: "I am speaking for Professor Endicott."

"Where is he?"

It was a woman's voice, but unlike the woman we had heard before. Slow and soft, almost languid. No hoarseness.

"He told me to tell anyone who called that he is at his bank now," I went on.

"Oh?"

31

"And that he will be back shortly."

"How soon is shortly?"

I had to improvise now. "Probably less than an hour."

Should I leave it at that?

No, I must emphasize the message. "He will be sorry to have missed you. I know he was expecting a call that meant a great deal to him, but he had to go to the bank when he did. There was no other way. May I tell him you will call again at seven?"

There was a click. She had cut the connection.

I had bungled the whole thing. How could I face Adam and Isolda now? How could I face myself?

Was there anything I could do?

Nothing.

This time I did make a drink, a strong one. Just as I had foreseen, it had no more effect on me than water.

It was ten minutes of seven when Adam and Isolda got back. They had got the money, but not from the bank. The banker himself had lent it to Adam privately.

"We'll wait till seven-thirty," said Isolda. "Then we'll have to turn the whole thing over to the police. We can't go on like this."

"We'll go on as long as we have to." Adam tossed ten one-thousand-dollar bills on the dining-table. "I'm not going to the police while there's a shadow of hope that we can get Kate back quickly with this money."

It was only a little after seven when the telephone rang again.

Adam's side of the conversation was terse.

"Yes . . . Yes . . . I'm ready . . . I'll leave at once."

He put down the receiver in its cradle and began to fill his pockets with the cash. "If the police come around, stall them until I get back. And don't worry. We've got to assume that things are going to be all right. I'll pay, and Kate will be set free and everything will be just as it used to be again."

32

Only it won't. I didn't say the words out loud, but I was thinking them. Nothing can ever be just as it used to be anywhere, at any time.

I made a last effort to dissuade Adam from going alone.

"My car is like a thousand others. A driver at night is just a silhouette against the lights. They wouldn't identify me or see that I was following you."

"Oh, but they would, Sam. Only a policeman or a CIA man can get away with that sort of thing. It takes professional training and experience."

I said no more. I had gone as far as I could.

Isolda and I stood at a kitchen window, watching Adam's car turn right at the foot of the driveway going towards the Danbury Road. She suggested we have sandwiches instead of dinner and wait there for Adam together. I used fatigue as an excuse for going home.

"Then I'll stay here alone," she said. "Somebody has to be on deck until Adam gets back. There might be another telephone call."

"Does Clara know you're here?"

"No, but I did leave a note for her saying I might be late getting home, so she won't worry or sit up for me if she gets there before I do."

"I feel guilty about leaving you alone," I said.

"Don't. You must rest."

"Will you call me if you need me for anything?"

"Of course."

I could not tell her that there might not be any answer if she called in the next hour or so.

My car is a standard American make, dark, inconspicuous and a little shabby. The only precaution I took was to smear a little mud over the license plate so no one could read the number.

I knew a shortcut to the Danbury Road, close to the fork

33

where it met the road Adam had just taken. I was pretty sure Isolda would not guess what I was up to, not after my insisting so particularly that she call me as soon as Adam got back. No matter what he said, I couldn't let anyone as innocent as he was wander into a situation like this without some protection.

Following another car on country roads is not difficult in daylight when there is usually some traffic. It becomes much more difficult after dark, especially on back roads where there is hardly any traffic at all. To avoid being noticed by your quarry, you have to hang back when rounding a curve until he has rounded the one beyond. Then you have to speed up and try to catch a glimpse of his taillights just before he rounds the next one.

If you lose him, you can only fall back on probability as Bazeries did in breaking ciphers. Is your quarry likely to be heading for city lights? Take the next road that leads to a town. You could catch up with him before he gets there. Is he more likely to be going to the house of a friend? Cruise the residential roads. You may spot his car parked in a driveway.

In other circumstances, I might have enjoyed that night's drive. It was pleasant country: wooded hills, open fields, water meadows; houses few and far between, standing well back from the road.

By daylight that landscape looks innocent but now I was seeing it by the diminished light of a gibbous moon, the crippled moon that may have been primordial man's first symbol of evil. I knew these roads yet I had a sudden illusion that I had never been here before.

Psychology calls this the *jamais vu*, opposite of the *déjà vu*. It lasted only a moment, but it left an aftertaste, the uneasy suspicion that nothing we experience is ever quite what it seems.

I rounded another curve. No sign of Adam. The road was empty.

I brought my foot down on the gas pedal, unleashing a whole

herd of horses, and the car surged forward. As I rounded the next curve, I eased off on the gas a little. Still no sign of Adam.

When I rounded the third curve, I knew I had lost him.

I used words I had not had occasion to use since I was in Southeast Asia. I had not been defeated by the cunning or malice of another human being, just by my own brute stupidity. I was out of practice and was getting old. I should have realized both those things.

I looked up at the crooked moon and thought: Primordial man was right. You are the Devil. You took my mind off the road. Only for a few seconds but that was enough.

I drove around for quite a while looking for some sign of Adam's car in a driveway or a cart track, but there was nothing. I tried to think where I might set up a secret meeting place if I were a kidnapper, and after a few moments I remembered the old Delano place.

Adam had not been driving towards it when he left his own driveway, but they might have directed him by a roundabout route so no one watching him leave would know where he was going.

I found the Danbury Road again. After a few miles I left it for a lesser road. I went up a steep hill and down the other side. I turned right and then left.

I had to pass Adam's own house now. There were lights in every window, but no car in the driveway.

I turned left again. This was more lane than road, winding through meadows into the woods. I lost the sky under the trees, but I drove on by the dim glow of my parking lights. That was as inconspicuous as I could make myself.

There were soft shoulders at either edge of this rough road. I came to a fairly wide bay screened from the road by fir trees. I turned off the road and parked behind the trees. Once I had switched off the parking lights, no one would see my car from the road unless he was looking for it.

I locked doors and windows and went on by foot.

35

Moonlight gives poorer visibility than most people realize. I was not wearing anything bright and I was in shadow.

I halted at the edge of the woods. Alone, in the soft spring night and the silence, I could almost hear the earth breathing in its sleep. The moon was playing hide and seek with the clouds. As its light came and went, the shadows changed shape and position. That would make it all the harder for anyone to see me.

I could barely make out the shell of the derelict house, one shattered gable dark against the pale sky, broken windows empty as blind eyes.

There was no hint of any other living presence, yet there were other creatures there, field mice and moles, chipmunks and rabbits, foxes and deer. Species that have any acquaintance with man soon learn that he is The Enemy.

I waited fifteen minutes, timing myself by my watch. I didn't think any human being could be there that long without giving some sign of his presence to anyone who was watching and listening. An animal could, but not a man, unless he were asleep, and who would sleep in such a place?

As I became convinced that my caution was unnecessary, I began to feel as foolish as a man who steps aside to avoid an obstacle that isn't there.

Still moving quietly, just in case I was wrong, I walked beyond the trees across the wild grass to the front door.

It must have been a handsome house years ago. Now the heavy door leaned against the outside wall supported only by one of its hinges.

I stepped inside. The beam from my flashlight sent shadows dancing around a wide hallway with a stair curving like a fan unfurled. There was filth everywhere. The stench of stale garbage and dung and urine made my stomach heave. They had used the fireplace for everything.

It was so like the smell of war and death that it brought back

36

Vietnam. For a moment I could almost feel the heat again and the gritty red dust of the coastal roads in my nostrils.

My light fell on a heap of clothes on the other side of the room. I picked my way across empty beer cans, grapefruit rinds and a magazine called *Screw.* It was just a heap of clothes, not, as I had feared for a moment, a body.

There was no sign of Adam. I made sure by going into every room upstairs and down.

On the stairway I found a small plastic doll. Its single garment, a calico dress, was torn and dirty. Half its nylon hair had been savagely torn from its scalp on one side. I remembered then what Kate had said about hearing a child crying in this house.

Something glittered in the wan light from the moon.

It was a fine gold chain wound around the doll's neck. From it dangled a carnelian bead engraved with the Chinese characters for peace and longevity.

5

It was almost midnight when I reached the Endicott house again. It still blazed like a Christmas tree, with lights at every window.

I left my car at the edge of the road and walked up the path to the front porch. There I could hear a male voice—flat, insistent, cheerful. For a moment I thought Isolda had a visitor. Then I realized that the male presence was electronic. She was listening to the twelve o'clock news.

When I tapped on a window, she rose so abruptly that she knocked over the light chair where she had been sitting.

"Adam!" She wrenched the door open. "Darling, I—" Her face congealed when she saw me. Her voice dropped almost an octave. "Why are you here?"

It must have been an enormous strain for her to sit there alone all evening, knowing that something was happening, but not knowing what it was.

"May I come in?"

"Of course." She stepped back, opening the door wider.

I took my time shutting it. Now that I knew the bond between Adam and Isolda was closer than I had ever suspected, I hardly knew what to say to her.

"Any telephone calls here?"

"None." She knew something was wrong. "Have you heard from Adam?"

"No." I turned off the newscaster in midsentence. "Isolda, I have bad news."

"About Kate?" Her breath was so short now she had difficulty forming the words.

"About Adam."

"Tell me." It was no more than a whisper.

"I changed my mind about following him but after about thirty minutes I lost him. I have no idea where he is now."

"Oh, Sam . . ." It was a mourning sound.

"I know where they've been holding Kate: at the old Delano place. She's not there now."

"How do you know she was there?"

"I found these."

She caught her breath when she saw what was in my hand.

"A doll's house doll and that chain of Kate's!"

I put them back in my pocket.

"You'd better have a drink."

I went to the table and poured some of Adam's best brandy into glasses for her and myself.

"Oughtn't we to call the police? That chain is evidence."

I shook my head. "We'd better wait a little longer."

"Why?"

"Presumably Adam is now in the middle of paying off the kidnappers. He did promise them he would keep the police out of it. He would hardly thank us if we brought them in now while the Hashashin still have Kate."

"I know and yet . . ."

"The police would ask awkward questions. Where did Adam get the money? Where did you and I get our share of it?"

"Those questions aren't awkward. Adam would tell them he borrowed on a savings account and got an unsecured personal

39

loan from a banking friend. I'd tell them I borrowed on my Treasury Bills."

"Unfortunately I am not in a position to be so candid. I cannot possibly tell the police, or anyone else, where I got the money I gave Adam."

"Why not?"

"There are reasons that have nothing to do with Adam or Kate or you."

"And if the police question me about you?"

"Tell them the truth: You don't know where my share of the money came from."

"And if they question you?"

"We'll cross that bridge when—"

I stopped. On a back road as lonely as this you could always hear a car approaching.

Rob Roy heard it, too. His growl had just the tone of a man swearing under his breath.

Isolda was staring at me. "Police?"

Before I could answer her, we heard the tread of heavy boots outside the front door.

I had rather expected Captain Carew to show up some time tonight, but I had not expected him to bring with him a detail of five troopers and a swarthy stranger with shrewd eyes whom he introduced as: "Mr. Digby, FBI."

Adam's living-room was built about two hundred years ago as a one-room schoolhouse. It is large enough to swallow a grand piano and a chimney of enormous field stones and still look spacious, but these troopers were big men in uniforms that made the most of their height and breadth. The moment they walked into that room, the ceiling came down and the walls closed in.

"Is this a Federal case already?" I asked Digby.

"All kidnapping cases becomes Federal cases in twenty-four hours." Digby made me feel I had opened my game with an indefensibly weak gambit. "The law presumes kidnappers will have to take their victim across a state line in that time."

"I'm still allowed to ask questions." Carew's voice was more friendly than Digby's, but his first question was straight to the point. "Where is Adam Endicott?"

"I don't know."

Digby decided to change his manner. He became almost affable. "Don't think we are unsympathetic. We know that a parent who refused to deal with a kidnapper would be an unnatural parent and we know that in what we call hostage situations the closer the search comes, the higher the hostage death rate. So let's put it this way: We won't try to interfere with Adam Endicott tonight and we won't be rough on him when he gets back, but we must know where he is. We've been keeping an eye on him, but . . ."

"You've lost him?"

"Well . . . yes." Digby did not like admitting that.

I understood only too well how he felt. I suppose that's why I couldn't resist needling him.

"Rather careless of you, wasn't it?"

"These things happen." His voice was grainy. "Let's get back to the question: Where is he now?"

"I told you, I don't know."

"There are laws about obstructing the police in the execution of their duty."

"I am sure there are dozens of such laws. I still don't know where Adam Endicott is now."

Isolda had retired to a wing chair on one side of the fireplace where she was sitting in shadow. Now, as she leaned forward, firelight revealed the good tweed suit, the hair carefully dressed to look careless, the colorless lipstick and the absence of all jewelry, except a plain wrist-watch and the old wedding ring she still wore for sentimental reasons. She looked exactly what I suppose she was: a member in good standing of the old

41

Eastern Establishment which is losing so much of its power today.

I had never thought of her like that before, but then I had never seen her in a situation like this before.

Her cool, clear voice rounded out the impression. "He really does not know where Adam is, Mr. Digby, and neither do I. We were talking about it just before you came in."

Carew and Digby had little defense against the effortless assertion of superiority implicit in her manner. Isolda didn't just think she was privileged. She knew she was, and what one knows other people will accept.

"You're suggesting that Adam has gone secretly to meet the kidnappers and pay the ransom," she went on. "Can you blame him? If it were my own daughter, Clara, I'm sure I'd do the same thing. Wouldn't you?"

In a Venetian museum there is a famous old portrait of a Renaissance Cardinal, one eye wide open, the other narrowed, as if he were always taking aim. That was the way Digby's eyes looked now.

"How can I say?" he answered Isolda. "I have no children."

"If Adam is doing anything like that," she went on, "he would hardly tell anyone else where he was going, would he?"

"Possibly not."

Their eyes met and held for a moment. Digby was the first to look away. He rose.

One of the troopers opened the front door for him. Carew paused in the doorway to look back.

"I should appreciate it if you would let us know when Mr. Endicott gets home. That can't possibly endanger his daughter."

Isolda must have been holding her breath those last few moments. When the men filed out with professional stolidity and the door closed, she let out an audible sigh.

"Where's that drink you poured me?"

I took our glasses over to the table near her chair.

42

Rob Roy had been sleeping at her feet all the time the police were there. Now he woke with a start.

"What's the matter, boy?" I said. "They've gone."

But he trotted back to the front door and growled again.

"Aberdeen terriers have sharper ears than most other dogs," said Isolda. "But they can't discriminate. That's probably a raccoon or a fox."

I went to the door myself. It was what they call a "Dutch door" in New York State, which means that you can open the top half without opening the bottom half.

In the upper half of the door there was a small window, veiled with a white net curtain so that people standing on the porch could not see inside.

I lifted one corner of the curtain and looked out through the glass. No one on the porch. No one on the moonlit lawn. No one moving in the shadows under the catalpa trees.

But Robbie began to bark.

I dropped the curtain and turned back to Isolda. "Must be a raccoon. Quiet, Rob!"

Even after all this time what followed is still as vivid to me as if it had happened yesterday.

My memory is rather like a color television set that I can't turn off. It runs night and day in one corner of my mind whether I happen to be watching and listening or not. Now I have only to glance in that direction and I can still see Isolda sitting in Adam's living-room that May night in the midseventies and everything that happened then reenacting itself eternally with, or without, an audience.

Once more I am aware of my own weariness as I hand Isolda her glass of brandy. Once more I think how handsome and haggard she looks as she rests her head against the high back of the wing chair.

And then it comes—the sudden loud crash, the thin tinkle of splintering glass.

Robbie bursts into a frenzy of barking and claws at the front door. Isolda's arm jerks, knocking over the glass on the table at her elbow. Brandy soaks into the thick wool of the Turkish rug. The room begins to smell like a distillery. My own head jerks around in the direction of the noise.

We had not bothered to draw the curtains across the tall, old-fashioned sash windows in the front wall of the house. Their panes were black with night. To anyone standing outside, the brightly lit room must have been an easy target.

The upper pane of the window to the left of the front door was split by an enormous, star-shaped hole.

"They've come back," faltered Isolda. "Those people who took Kate."

I opened the door. Robbie darted down the lawn to the edge of the road, still barking.

There was no one I could see. There was nothing but the ragged clouds and the hunchbacked moon and the warm breath of the May night, soft against my cheek.

Beyond the trees, I heard a car starting in low gear. Someone shifted into high. The sound dwindled and died in the distance.

I called Robbie back inside and shut the door.

"Hit and run," I said.

"There's something on the floor," said Isolda. "By the window."

It's never easy to identify anything out of its context. I expected a brick or a stone. It took me a second or so to realize that I was holding a tape cassette as well as a stone. The two were tied together and wrapped in a piece of old newspaper. I crumpled the paper and stuffed it in one of my pockets.

"Does Adam have a machine that will play a Sony tape?"

"In his study. I'll get it."

The only table near an electric socket was a taboret of natural teak from Thailand, a gift to Adam from his Vietnamese students when he left Hué.

44

I pushed the plug in the socket and turned on the switch. The soft, slow voice of the woman I had heard on the telephone began to speak.

"This is a second message from the Task Force of the New Hashashin. The next voice you hear will be the voice of our Beloved Leader and Lord High Commander, Hassan-ben-Sabah."

A pause, then the deep voice of the man we had heard before. This time it was an angry voice.

"What you trying to do, Adam Endicott? When we called just after six, like we said we would, you weren't there. So we give you a second chance. We call back later. We tell you where to meet us and what happens? You don't show up.

"You playing games? This isn't a game.

"How you think your daughter feels now she knows you missed a telephone call and a meeting? She's beginning to wonder if she means anything at all to you. So are we.

"You setting up a trap for us? You'll be sorry if you do. Did you go to a bank for the money? There's a black market for money. That's quicker and we're in a hurry.

"I guess all you care about is money. Even your daughter is just one of your possessions you want to buy back at bargain rates, not somebody you care about.

"So you listen to me, Adam Endicott: This is your last chance. If you're not at that place we told you in the next hour you're not going to see your daughter again. She's okay now. We been nice to her. We don't beat people or brainwash them. No, sir!

"She's so happy here with us she is not sure she wants to go back to you now. How do you like that? She's beginning to see through you. She's beginning to think you're a fake. If you don't show up with the money this time, she's going to know you're a fake. She's going to know you don't give a damn about what happens to her.

45

"You don't believe that? Okay, I'm going to let her speak for herself now. But don't you get funny ideas. We didn't hurt her. We didn't brainwash her. She's changed all by herself. And how! Just wait till you hear her. You listen careful. This is the way she is now."

A girl's voice followed, gabbling faster than I had ever heard Kate speak, the words all slurred and melded as if she had taken drink or drugs. Even more uncharacteristic was the tone: petulant, querulous, scolding.

"Father, you don't really care about me at all, do you? If you did, you'd have got the money by this time and I'd be free. I don't think you understand these people who are holding me as a hostage. They're not criminals. They're just concerned about the state of the world and determined to do something about it. They don't have money enough for that, so they have to get it from people like you.

"Don't think of me as being kidnapped. Think of me as being captured in a civil war and held for ransom, the way kings and knights were in the Middle Ages.

"I don't suppose you understand any of this. You've spent your whole life lecturing at universities for the sons of rich men and getting the fathers to finance your archaeological expeditions. What do you know or care about the disinherited of this earth? Have you ever missed a meal in your whole life because you couldn't pay for it?

"There's one thing I must make clear. These people have not brainwashed me or terrorized me or bullied me to make me say things like this. They've talked to me and lent me books to read and opened my eyes to many things. I'm not the person I was. I see you and your kind now as you really are: exploiters of the weak and defenseless who are the majority of people on this earth. I am now a member of the New Hashashin and proud of it.

"So please don't grudge them the money they want. They're

going to do good with it. And please get it for them quickly. Father, I do want to see you again, but if there are any more delays I never will . . ."

The man's voice came back.

"Well, Adam Endicott? You heard her. She means every word she says and she has not been brainwashed so you better act fast. You don't get another chance and neither will she.

"End of message."

I saw tears running down Isolda's cheeks yet her face was blank and she was not making a sound. This is the most awful kind of crying when the will remains in control of face and voice but the tear glands, dissociated and uncontrollable, weep as mechanically as a leaky faucet.

I put a hand on her shoulder. "Don't."

"This will kill Adam." She spoke as if she were stunned. "Unless . . . was that Kate's voice? Could they have killed her already and put a changeling in her place?"

6

The flames in the fireplace had died down. Now there was only a heap of powdery ash with here and there a red gleam from a slow-burning ember under the surface.

I broke the silence.

"Haven't those damned whores been guillotined yet?"

I achieved my purpose. Isolda was startled out of her shock.

"What are you talking about?"

"An eight-year-old King, Louis the Seventeenth, of France. The women to whom he referred as whores were his mother, aunt and young sister. The sudden transformation of his mind and character is a classic case of brainwashing that occurred long before the word was invented."

"But she said she had not been brainwashed. The man said it, too."

"Yes, he said it three times, didn't he? Too often."

"Louis the Seventeenth was noted for his family affection. He clung to his mother, aunt and sister when he kissed them goodbye. He was dragged away, sobbing: 'Don't let them take me!' For three days afterward his mother could hear him crying. Then silence.

"Drugs were not commonly available then, so the child was kept on brandy. He was taught the coarse vocabulary of hate and a lawyer's questions tricked him into accepting a charge of incest against his mother and himself.

"He laughed when he answered the questions, sitting in an armchair, swinging little legs too short to reach the floor.

"After his mother was put to death, he was placed in solitary confinement. For a year and five months he was kept in a cramped closet with little light, no fresh air or exercise. His unmade bed crawled with lice and fleas. Food was brought him in silence. Soon he would not, or could not, speak to anyone. The few sightseers who saw him then could not believe that this filthy, half-witted, rachitic child had once been the Dauphin of France. Doctors said that if he had survived he would have been an imbecile all his life."

"So he died?"

"He disappeared," I told her. "And his body was never found. Don't you understand that brainwashing is much older than Pavlov and Freud? They invented theories to explain it, but they didn't invent the thing itself.

"Remember Caspar Hauser, a youth who suddenly appeared on a road near Nuremberg in the eighteenth century? An appearance can be just as mysterious as a disappearance. He was so physically and mentally crippled that doctors say he must have been confined in some sort of tiger-cage all his life and conditioned to forget his own history.

"Remember the Janissaries? Christian children captured in war by Islamic Turks and brought up in such fanatic devotion to Islam they became the fiercest of all Islamic fighters against Christian communities?"

"But it takes years to produce effects like that," protested Isolda.

"That's not the opinion of Brian Jenkins, who has made a study of political violence. There are certain bonds between kidnapper and hostage. First, they both want the demands to be met, especially the hostage whose life depends on it. Then both sides discover that it is hard to talk to anyone for days, or even hours, and not see something of the other's point of view.

"The hostage knows, perhaps unconsciously, that he must move out of the category of a thing to be bargained with and become a human being to the captive. It's a little harder for them to kill a human being. So he whiles away the dreary waiting time by asking them about their lives and telling them about himself, and they respond. They become human, too. This is the fraternization feared and hated by all war leaders who want to get on with the war.

"But the thing that breaks down the hostage sooner or later is his knowledge that his captors may kill him at their whim whether demands are met or not. The captors are omnipotent, gods with absolute power of life and death before whom the hostage is helpless, frightened, humiliated, virtually an infant. Under these circumstances the hostage unconsciously begins to assimilate—and even imitate—the attitudes of his captors."

"I've never heard of this Mr. Jenkins," said Isolda. "But I know that some psychologists say there is no such thing as brainwashing. They say that American war prisoners who claim they were brainwashed in Korea or North Vietnam are liars. They were so lightly guarded they could have escaped if they had really wanted to."

When people who have never been in prison or combat start laying down the law about such things, it irritates me. I managed to keep the irritation out of my voice.

"Isn't that the point? That something killed their wanting to?"

"You mean they were all treated like Caspar Hauser?"

"We have drugs to speed up the process today. Even without drugs, we've learned to use the techniques first invented to build up shattered minds for tearing down normal minds."

"Inverted analysis?"

"It's been known to break terrorists themselves when a police siege turns them into prisoners."

"Nothing will break a man with character and faith in his own cause."

"Oh, Isolda! 'Before the cock crow, thou shalt deny me thrice.'"

"What could those Hashashin gain by forcing Kate to repudiate Adam?"

"Everything. It is a masterstroke of propaganda, worthy of Goebbels. Liberals have been dissociating themselves from political kidnappers. That has to be stopped or the kidnappers cannot go on posing as humanitarian, liberal crusaders. What better way to stop it than by announcing the kidnapping victim's voluntary conversion to her kidnappers' ideology?

"At one blow the victim forfeits public sympathy, press and public are made to feel they have been hoaxed and the kidnapping itself becomes a victimless crime. Whether she wishes to or not, she is now locked into an association with the Hashashin which she can never escape. How would Alice have felt on the other side of her Looking Glass if the Red Queen had sealed the glass so Alice could never find her way home again?"

Isolda lifted her brandy to her lips. Her hand was shaking now.

"So blows or drugs, electric shocks or hypnosis can make a traitor out of anybody?"

"Not just blows or drugs, hypnosis or electric shocks."

"What then?"

"Lack of a place to sit or lie or stand, lack of food and water and cleanliness, fresh air and exercise. Lack of rest and sleep and the dreams which are so necessary to mental health. Lack of hope and companionship. The human personality is more fragile than most people have any idea."

"But if you really believe in something . . ."

"What is belief? Creeds in conflict are opposites. Conversion is really inversion, turning the mind inside out, a mechanical process, easier than you think."

"Then you can rape the mind as well as the body?"

"It's an old human custom to rape both."

She looked at me as desperately as a lone swimmer who suddenly finds herself beyond her depth with no help near.

"Sam, do you know what it is like to be at the mercy of someone who may kill you at any moment?"

"I was in Vietnam. Remember?"

"But not in the Army . . . or were you?"

I almost told her then. I pulled back just in time. Isolda Marriott was the last person in the world I wanted to confide in and I am sure I was the last person in the world whose confession she would want to hear.

The fact that we had suddenly come so close to an intimacy neither of us wanted showed how our normal behavior was breaking down under stress.

I mumbled that newspaper men hear about many things they don't experience themselves. She pretended to accept that though I am sure she didn't really.

"Shouldn't we call the police now?" I went on. "They'll have to hear this tape."

"I think we should wait until Adam gets back," she answered. "He should be here any moment now and he may not want the police to hear the tape yet."

I rose. "Then let's play the damned thing again. There may be something significant in it that we missed the first time."

I turned the volume high. We were halfway through when Robbie growled.

"Quiet!" I spoke more sharply than I usually speak to a dog. I was trying to concentrate so hard on every inflection of the voice that might or might not be Kate's that I didn't notice any sound on the porch until I heard a knock.

"May I come in?"

It was Carew, alone this time.

The voice on the tape was loud and clear. "Taking hostages is the only way they can—"

Isolda switched it off, but she wasn't quite quick enough.

"What is that?" demanded Carew.

I answered as if it were unimportant. "A tape recording."

"Is it a telephone call from the kidnappers?"

"No. It's a cassette that was thrown through the window a little while ago."

"Oh?" His glance went to the star-shaped hole in the glass. "From the kidnappers?"

"Yes. Addressed to Adam Endicott, but he hasn't heard it yet. We're expecting him at any moment."

"It's a recording of a girl's voice," added Isolda. "She identifies herself as Kate, but the voice does not sound like Kate's voice to me."

I expected this to fire Carew's interest, but he surprised me.

He didn't rush to the telephone. He scarcely looked at the tape recorder. He merely sat down in the nearest chair with something like a sigh.

"You're tired." There was surprise in Isolda's voice as if she had always assumed that policemen never got tired. "It is late," she added, justifying him politely.

"Would a drink help?" I asked him.

"Thank you. I'll break a self-imposed rule and have a little of that brandy you're drinking even if I am on duty."

He sipped in silence.

Isolda was the first to suspect the truth. "Something else has happened?"

"Yes."

A wild hope flared in me. "You've found Kate?"

"No, Mr. Joel. We've found Adam Endicott. His car is standing on the bridge down the road without lights. He is sitting in the driver's seat and there's a bullet hole in his forehead. He's been dead for at least an hour, probably longer."

7

When you are having a nightmare you sometimes know that it's just a dream, that in a few moments you will wake in another, saner world.

That was how I felt when I woke Monday morning. I looked around at my dreary little bedroom, with its skimpy, drip-dry curtains, and I knew none of this was real. It was just a dream and, in a few moments, I would wake in another, saner world.

But this time the nightmare wouldn't go away. There would be no waking in a saner world. This was the only world there was.

Would it have been better if I had not followed Adam last night? Could they have killed him because they saw he was not alone? I had kept so far behind Adam no one could possibly have seen that I was following him. That was why I had lost him. Perhaps he would have been safer if I had stayed closer to him so it could have been seen that he was not alone.

I took an ice-cold shower, something I usually avoid. I ate a hearty breakfast, something I didn't want. Still, I felt as if I were walking in a dream.

The sun was just rising as I finished breakfast. I played television roulette until a news program came up. It was all about the history of patricide, the sort of thing newspaper men write when an editor asks them to follow up a story and there is nothing new they can use in following up.

The speaker obviously believed Kate had conspired with her apparent kidnappers to kill her father. That was the effect the tapes had on most people. They simply could not believe that the Hashashin could force Kate to make such tapes against her will.

He ended with an ominous line: "Kate Endicott can never come home now for she has eaten the pomegranate seed."

At first, I couldn't place the allusion. Then it came back to me. When Pluto carried off Persephone to Hades, she knew that, if she ate pomegranate seed there, she could never go home to live again with her mother, Ceres.

It was too early for newspapers or mail and much too early to go to any of the places where I wanted to go, but there was one thing I could do: look through the library at the big house for books about the ancient Hashashin of the Middle East.

When I put on the jacket I had worn last night, I found something in the right-hand pocket which I had forgotten: the half-sheet of crumpled newspaper that had been wrapped around the cassette and stone when they were tossed through the window. I was about to drop it in a scrapbasket when a dateline caught my eye.

Sphinx, New York, May 26, 1976.

Long ago Park Row was the newspaper street in New York as Broadway is still the theater street. *Sphinx* was an "off-Park Row newspaper," published in the East Village.

I scanned the clipping for marked paragraphs or anything else of significance.

All I found was a scrap of paper pasted to the newsprint. It looked as if it were part of a mailing label that had included the subscriber's name and address, but it was torn in half and all that remained was the name of a news agent rubber-stamped in purple ink and so blurred I could only just make out the words: *Lamborn Street News Agency.* At least that address was a little more specific than just East Village.

I put the paper back in my pocket and walked down the driveway through the early morning sunshine to the big house.

Built in the heyday of the great predators, it was a handsome monument to their conspicuous waste in the exuberant Beaux Arts style of its period. It was ample enough to be regarded as a minor chateau in France, but, for all its heroic scale and lavish use of precious materials, it had no future here. As soon as the present owner died, the bulldozers would move in. Even clubs and private schools could not afford the taxes now, and the fashion in individual homes was for places that looked like sets for *Star Trek.*

I unlocked the front door, a slab of oak with carved panels, and crossed a great hall. I passed through a white and gold drawing-room with a white bearskin rug and a white piano, and a black and gold drawing-room, with a black bearskin rug and a black piano. I lingered a moment in a small morning-room, in the Petit Trianon style, all printed cottons from Jouy-en-Josas, and finally came to the library.

It, too, was furnished with the best work of the best cabinet-makers made in their best periods, but somehow it was less self-conscious than the other rooms. Had it been less frequented and so received less attention?

No matter what the time of day I always felt as if I were seeing its Islamic rugs by candlelight. That was the soft glow of the vegetable dyes, found only in old rugs.

There were four walls of books beginning with the poetic prose of the eighteenth century and ending with the prosaic poetry of the twentieth century. History was represented liberally and I found three books that looked promising.

The first was *Secret Societies of the Middle Ages,* a "new" edition published in 1848 without the author's name. Someone had pencilled it in on the title page: "Thos. Keightley."

The second was *Secret Fraternities of the Middle Ages* with a less modest author. Not only were we told his name and status, Americo Palfrey Morros, B.A., late of Lincoln College, but we were also informed that this book had won the Arnold Prize and had been read aloud in the Theatre, Oxford, on June 21st, 1865.

The third, *Famous Secret Societies*, by John Heron Lepper, London, 1932, was the only one of real value to the modern reader.

I was deep in the deadly machinations of Hassan-ben-Sabah, Sheikh al Jebal, when I heard a footstep in the small morning-room.

I moved quietly to the library door and opened it a few inches.

Joey Alfieri stood just inside the door, bare feet wide apart, hands on hips, throat stretched as he looked up at the carved beams and painted plaster in the faraway ceiling.

"Wow! I never saw a place like this before in my life. Did people actually live here once?"

"One of them still does. He's in Morocco now."

Joey's gaze swept to the one door that led to the other rooms. "Two grand pianos. Two bearskin rugs. I can't believe it. How many rooms on this floor?"

"I have no idea."

"You live here and you don't know?"

"I haven't bothered to check the inventory. Did you come here to see me?"

"Yeah. You weren't at your little house, but your car was in the driveway, so I thought you might be over here. The door was open and I just walked in. Clara's still at your place."

"Then let's go back there."

Joey watched as I locked the front door and reset the combination on the alarm system.

"Security?"

"My job here."

As usual when I came back from the big house my own place seemed to have shrunk to the dimensions of a rabbit hutch. Even the terrace looked hardly bigger than a handkerchief.

Clara sat on its edge, skinny legs dangling. She is so lean and tall that she looks elongated rather than big, like a reflection in a trick mirror. She is watercolor fair, silver-blond hair, lavender-blue eyes, pink and white skin, but this morning her whole face was red and swollen and wet with tears.

"It's all so awful," she cried. "And this is the last straw."

"What is?"

"Robbie."

I hadn't noticed the dog. When he heard his name, he came forward. I leaned down to scratch his head. "He looks all right."

"Oh, he looks all right, but . . ." Clara found a tight, damp wad of paper tissue and wiped her eyelids. "You see I can't take Robbie back to New York with me. I'm out all day at the office."

"And I can't take him back to college," said Joey. "No pets allowed."

I looked at Clara. "Surely your mother . . .?"

"That's what I thought, but she won't."

I sat down beside Clara and Joey squatted on his heels beside us. "Why not?" I demanded.

"It's these news broadcasts. Every time she listens to one, she changes."

Joey jumped up. "You got a TV? It's just about time for news now."

We went inside my postage-stamp living-room. Like everything else there, the set had come with the house. It was small and shabby, but it worked well enough. I turned it on and we got the tail-end of a Washington economist telling us there was nothing to worry about, fiscal prospects had never been brighter. . . .

". . . and now the latest developments in the Katie Endicott case."

The next face on the screen was Digby's. I hadn't noticed the fine lines in his dry lips before, but then I had never seen his face so close before.

A newscaster was speaking offscreen. "We now bring you Clarence Digby, who is leading the hunt for Katie Endicott."

Just after the kidnapping reporters, police and FBI had all referred to Kate as "Miss Endicott" or "Katherine Endicott." Now she was just "Katie." A little thing? Perhaps, but still an indication of diminishing respect.

Digby's voice sounded the way you imagine a computer's voice would sound if a computer could talk, but that may have been just microphone distortion.

"People keep asking us if we are sure that the girl's voice on the tapes is really Katie's voice," he said. "I can announce now that we are absolutely sure. Voice-print analysis has established beyond all reasonable doubt that the voice is Katie's. This morning we discovered further evidence, a Polaroid photograph in a letter from the Hashashin apparently mailed to Professor Endicott before his death to prove to him once and for all that the girl in their custody is Katie.

"Their letter calls attention to the fact that, far from her being threatened or coerced in any way, the girl in the photograph is actually carrying a gun. This is offered as proof that she is no longer a captive, but now an active supporter of the New Hashashin.

"Since the girl's identity is a pivotal question in this case, we are now going to show this photograph on television in the hope that everyone who knew Katie will now come forward and and confirm the identification."

Again I had that dreamlike feeling: This is not happening. In a few minutes I will wake up. But I didn't.

The photograph was more damning than the voice on the tape. Image is the basic tool of human thought. Our very word for creative thinking is "imagination" and the effect of a picture on us is always powerfully suggestive, almost hypnotic.

I tried to resist that suggestion and ask myself objectively: Is this Kate or isn't it?

I could see a resemblance, but, if it was she, how chillingly she had changed.

In only thirty-six hours she had lost weight. For the first time I could see bones in her face and neck. They made her look older. Only anxiety and fasting together can cause such a great loss of weight in so short a time.

Her mouth, that had always curved so gently, was now set in the hard straight line of fear. Worst of all were her eyes, darkly desperate. Did the Hashashin really think this photograph would establish that she was happy with them?

The big ugly gun she held so awkwardly was a gross incongruity, like a coarse word scrawled across a work of art.

The picture vanished. Digby's face came back. Another voice, offscreen, was interviewing him.

"I take it, Mr. Digby, that you no longer regard Katie as a simple victim of kidnapping?"

"How can we? No matter what she was in the beginning she, herself, is now alleging that she joined the New Hashashin voluntarily while they were engaged in a conspiracy to extort money from her father which led to his death. No trace of ransom money was found on his body or in his car, which makes the motive crystal clear. Conspiracy and extortion are felonies and homicide in the commission of a felony is murder in the first degree. In some states that still calls for the death penalty.

"We are therefore sending out posters with Katie's photograph and description for display in all post offices throughout the country saying that she is wanted on suspicion of murdering her own father."

I heard a sob from Clara. Joey muttered something about

lynching people on television. I kept my eyes on the screen.

The interviewer was still talking.

"Is it true, Mr. Digby, that you are now trying to establish in which of several neighboring states Professor Endicott was actually killed?"

"Yes. A state that still has the death penalty would be a good spot."

I shall always wonder why Digby made such an extraordinary remark in public. Afterward somebody must have warned him that he had gone too far for he never said anything like that again, but, in that one unguarded moment, he had revealed an animus against Kate unbecoming in a law enforcement officer.

Of course he didn't know the real, flesh and blood girl I knew and loved. To him Kate was probably not a girl at all, but merely a symbol of everything he thought was wrong with contemporary society.

I don't remember the rest of the interview. The next thing I recall is a new voice offscreen saying: "We now take you to a neighbor of the Endicotts, Mrs. Marriott."

"Oh, no!" cried Clara.

Joey reached for her hand and held it tight.

As the camera lens picked up Isolda's ravaged face, she was shaking her head.

"No. I have nothing to say. Please."

The camera drew back a little and I saw that she was standing on her own doorstep. I suppose they had caught her by ringing the doorbell and focusing the lens on her the moment she opened the door.

"Just one question, Mrs. Marriott!"

The faceless, offscreen voice galloped over the words, determined to get the question in before the door was slammed.

"Do you regard Katie Endicott as a victim of crime or as a criminal herself?"

Isolda's hand, halfway to the doorknob, paused.

"She's a wanton, vicious criminal who deserves the death penalty."

The door closed.

The interviewer's face came back on screen now, a large, fleshy face that matched the chatty, jovial voice.

". . . and public opinion is still divided. The majority seems to be siding with Mrs. Marriott, but, in southern California, some cars are carrying bumper stickers that read: WE LOVE YOU, KATIE, and . . ."

Joey looked at me in bewilderment. "I don't get it. Who are they and why do they love her?"

"They'd probably call themselves radicals," I answered him. "But I'd call them romantics. They have taken Kate's confession at face value for, if they accept the idea of a forced confession, they lose their image of the Hashashin as crusading idealists. If Kate ever repudiates her conversion publicly, they will turn on her. There is one thing romantics cannot bear—losing their illusions.

"The fascinating thing is that their ideological opposite, Digby, also has to take Kate's conversion at face value for, if he doesn't, he'll lose his image of Kate as a menace to society. Neither the right nor the left see her as a human being any more. She is just one of the counters in their endless game."

"That's horrible." Joey spoke as if he had never thought of the case in those terms before.

I went on: "For many people it isn't Kate who's on trial. It's the whole younger generation. Of course that isn't fair to Kate, but there is so much juvenile crime today that the old and even the middle-aged are beginning to hate as well as fear the young."

"And there is so much adult corruption and abuse of power that the young are beginning to hate as well as fear the old and the middle-aged," said Clara. "Kate is my best friend and now my own mother is helping to lynch her."

"Is there no way we can get her out of this, Mr. Joel?" asked Joey.

I turned off the television, which was beginning to make any talk difficult.

"It may be too late, Joey. Have you thought of that?"

"What do you mean?"

"We have to face it. Kate may be dead already. The photograph and the tapes could have been made before she was killed."

It took Joey a moment to collect himself.

"Do you really think that, Mr. Joel?"

"There's only one thing I'm sure of: Kate had nothing to do with killing her father."

"And she might still be alive?" insisted Clara.

"It's possible."

"You are going to do something about it, aren't you?" cried Joey.

"I'm thinking about that."

"The police said we were too young to help, but you'll let us know if there's anything we can do, won't you?"

"Of course." A flat lie. I agreed with the police.

When they had gone I moved swiftly, packing a small, battered suitcase that I had had for years. There was a compartment concealed in the lid cunningly enough to get by the casual search of customs officers who had no reason to suspect anything wrong, but unlikely to escape a serious search by police, CIA or crooks. I kept a passport there, always up to date, and ten thousand in cash which I never touched except for real emergencies.

I decided the slacks and jacket I was wearing were shabby enough to pass muster where I was going, but I changed my shoes for an older pair that were scuffed and run down at the heels. Fortunately my raincoat needed cleaning. It looked quite disreputable enough to be exactly what I wanted.

63

I had to leave my other clothes and my income tax records for the last three years, the period for which you are legally accountable. I had to leave my radio and tape recorder. They looked too expensive. I didn't even think of taking my razor. I hesitated over my typewriter, the smallest, lightest brand on the market, but finally decided against it. I could always rent a typewriter.

When I was ready to go, I had nothing with me but the small suitcase, the raincoat and the clothes I stood up in. I couldn't even take my watch. Where I was going it would be a dead giveaway.

And I couldn't take Robbie.

I looked down at him. "Sorry, boy. You can't come, but there's a vet in Fairfield who'll take good care of you."

He wagged his tail slowly in that way he had which expressed politeness rather than enthusiasm. He knew perfectly well that something was wrong. Was it just my tone of voice?

He didn't even bark when I heard a car outside.

I went to the door.

Convertibles are going out of fashion and it was a long time since I had seen one as showy as this. It was almost white with a latent, greenish cast that echoed the dark green of the leather upholstery.

A youth vaulted over the door without bothering to open it. He was dressed for tennis in white which set off his blond coloring, but what really held the eye was the symmetrical figure and the graceful movement. His face was plain, almost ugly, but he needed that touch of asymmetry to give him humanity.

He was smiling now, but the smile didn't reach his eyes. They were troubled.

"Mr. Joel? I'm Neil Ormsby."

That told me a lot. This was the Neil Kate had mentioned who went to Yale. His family had inherited another big house like this one. They were living in theirs.

He went on: "I've come to see you because I know you are a friend of Kate Endicott's. So am I."

"I've heard of you."

"Really? I don't know Kate too well. I've been hoping I'd get to know her better this summer." His eyes opened wide. "Why, you've got Robbie!"

"And Robbie didn't bark when you arrived. That's a sort of introduction."

"Not with Robbie. I'd have to attack you before he protested."

So he knew Kate well enough to know Robbie's character.

I invited him onto the terrace and offered him coffee or beer. He chose coffee.

"I am . . . very fond of Kate." He was looking down as he spoke, a little embarrassed.

I might have known then there would be at least one young man like this somewhere in Kate's life by this time, one older and more experienced than the Joeys of this world.

He lifted unhappy eyes to mine.

"I've talked to the police. They say there is nothing I can do to help them."

"They're probably right."

"I understand you've been in this thing from the beginning and everybody says you care about Kate. Are you going to do anything about it?"

"I'm going to try."

"Can you tell me about it?"

"No."

"Is there anything I can do to help you?"

"Perhaps. I'm going away for a while."

"I thought you had a newspaper job here."

"I've got a month's leave of absence. If that runs out before I'm ready, I'll let the job go."

Some people would have warned me about the importance of hanging on to a job. This never occurred to Neil Ormsby.

65

He belonged to a world where jobs were something you took on for fun.

"I have a second job," I went on. "I'm caretaker of this place and I've been worrying for fear I may not be able to find a replacement."

"I'll take it on myself," said Neil promptly.

"Are you willing to sleep here? That's part of it."

"Why not? It's a nice old place."

"Another thing: Rob Roy. I hate to leave him with a vet for what may be a long time."

Neil smiled again. It was a pleasant smile even when he was not happy. "I'll be glad of Robbie's company. How am I going to keep in touch with you? Just in case something comes up?"

"You can't. I'll be moving around. So I'll have to keep in touch with you."

I handed him the house keys and the combination for the alarm system and said goodbye to Robbie.

Neil followed me down the path to my car. I was turning on the ignition when he said: "Would it be out of line to ask just one more question?"

"You can't be shot for asking."

"Where are you going?"

I hesitated for only a moment, then I said:

"Underground."

As I went down the driveway, I could see him in my rear-view mirror, gazing after the car. He was no longer smiling. He was remarkably thoughtful.

I picked up the Merritt Parkway on Sport Hill Road and I had got as far as Stamford when suddenly it hit me.

Such thoughts usually come to us only in the watches of the night when we should be sleeping. That's why they are called "night thoughts," but this one came to me in broad daylight.

I pulled over into the right lane so I could drive more slowly.

Doubt is the shadow of faith. You cannot have one without

the other, but there are some doubts you can never share with anyone else. This was one.

I loved Kate, but . . . what does one human being ever really know about another?

Suppose I was wrong about her. Suppose she had wanted to join the Hashashin all along and had connived at her own kidnapping in order to do so? Suppose she had stood aside without protest while they killed her father?

I moved back into the left lane, so I could drive faster.

PART TWO

Defeat

And the Piper advanced, and the children followed,
And, when all were in to the very last,
The door in the mountainside shut fast . . .

Browning, *The Pied Piper of Hamelin*

8

I spent my first two hours in the East Village wandering about Lamborn Street bars and coffee shops, listening and observing and occasionally joining in conversation. The Endicott case was widely discussed, but I gleaned no information I didn't have already, except the fact that an off-Broadway theater was coining money by exploiting the obviously humorous aspects of such a comic situation as this kidnapping.

I heard no voices that sounded like those on the tapes. The Lamborn Street News Agency said what I expected them to say: They had a great many *Sphinx* subscribers and they could not possibly identify any one of them from the scrap of paper in my possession.

I was not disappointed because I had not really expected anything from this first exploration of the neighborhood.

It was from a bartender on Lamborn Street that I got the address of a place to live.

I won his sympathy by telling him I had been looking over personals in *Sphinx* and even the single rooms there were too expensive for me. I was now in an inverted neighborhood where the poorer you are the more sympathetically you are treated. If I had been silly enough to say that I was looking for a place a little nicer than those advertised in *Sphinx* I would have got a very cold stare accompanied by some disagreeable remarks about the sexual habits of my ancestors.

As it was the bartender said: "Let me think a minute."

I bought him a beer to lubricate his thinking.

After a few moments of trancelike abstraction, he came to life with a glad cry: "Potter's Field! That's the place for you!"

I laughed. "I may look dead, but—"

"Na-a, we just call it that. The real name is Potter's Alley. Go to the guy who runs the deli on the corner and tell him you want a place at Number 123. You can get a pad there for practically nothing."

"What's wrong with it?"

"Not much." He looked at me a little more closely. "Not everybody would want to go there, but you did ask for something dirt cheap. Here, I'll write it down for you."

He dug a blunt stub of pencil out of a pocket and tore a narrow strip off the margin of my copy of *Sphinx*. He wrote slowly and laboriously: *123 Potter's Alley.*

"Who owns the place? The guy who runs the deli?"

"Na-a, he just collects rent. Some bank maybe got it for a bad debt."

I had left my car at a garage in Stamford. I didn't expect to see it again until this was over. It was not enough just to look and talk poor. I must be poor if I were going to melt into the landscape of the Village. So taxis were out.

My map told me that there was no subway or bus that would take me near Potter's Alley. I would have to walk and it was going to be a long walk.

I was struggling through a street lined with loft buildings and choked with trucks loading and unloading when I discovered that I was being followed.

I had expected this might happen but I had not expected it so soon.

A few minutes later I turned a corner and came upon Potter's Alley suddenly.

Poverty is as relative as everything else. There are black holes of privation in the Far East that are physically worse than Potter's Alley, but I know of no place where I have felt a deeper sense of deprivation. Was it because our people have been taught to expect more for so long and have been so often disappointed? Which is really important, the way things are or the way we feel about them?

It was a narrow street of old yellow-brick tenement houses containing cold-water flats. The front doors stood open day and night. Inside were vestibules with rows of doorbells. Theoretically you had to ring a bell to gain entrance to any room upstairs. Practically anyone could walk upstairs at any hour of the day or night and pick a cheap lock or force a flimsy door with a few blows. Ideas like privacy and safety did not exist here.

On every roof there was a thicket of television aerials sprouting in all directions like hairs growing out of a wart. This was the one luxury, the one window on the outside world. Here people would go without necessities to pay for that luxury.

On a warm spring afternoon like this there were people in the street and on the front steps. One man was mending a broken ground-floor window with Scotch Tape. An old woman sat on a door step painting her nails with silver varnish. Two little girls on the sidewalk played a game with a bouncing ball and jacks. A few half-grown boys were tossing a football back and forth in the middle of the street. This was a dead end where cars were rare.

You could hardly use the old Venetian word "ghetto" here. This was not a place where people of one race or culture were segregated by law or custom. This was an old-fashioned slum where the only thing people had in common was their poverty.

The old woman was white. The little girls were black. The boys had skins of many shades from ivory to brown and they were using both Spanish and English words.

Everyone stopped speaking when I appeared, but no one

73

looked up. This was a place where strangers were regarded with more caution than curiosity. Everyone became suddenly extra busy with whatever he or she was doing. They did not even talk to one another now.

The silence was eerie, eloquent of alienation and controlled hostility.

As soon as I saw Number 123 I understood why rooms there would be dirt cheap.

It was a lone survivor of the eighteen-sixties or seventies, a squat little, three-storey frame house squeezed so tight between two taller tenements that it looked as if it were being crushed physically. There was no porch or stoop. Its front door opened directly on the street at street level.

It must have stood empty for a long time. Every window was smashed. One of the two front steps was broken. Its clapboard walls were so weathered and dirty, so scabbed and scaly, it was impossible to tell what color the paint had been originally.

I doubted if the man at the deli had any legal right to collect rent. No bank owned this house. Some private landlord must have abandoned it years ago because he could no longer make it pay for its taxes and it had been derelict ever since.

I tried the front door. As I expected, it opened. I stepped into a narrow hall with a steep stair. I had expected the dirt and the stale smells inside. I had not expected the curious feeling that the silence in the street had followed me indoors.

It took only a few minutes to go through the little house. On each floor there were two cold-water flats, each consisting of a combined bathroom and kitchen, with the bathtub adjoining the sink, and a combined bedroom and living-room. There were no closets. There was an old-fashioned water-closet in the hallway on each floor. All the rooms were unfurnished. No one had lived here for a long time except the rats who had left their droppings on the floors.

I decided that the second-floor back would suit me best. The ground floor was a little too vulnerable to the street and the attic floor a little too high for a jump to the ground in case of fire or other emergency. Apparently the former landlords had never heard of fire regulations for there was no sign of a fire escape anywhere.

Outside the back windows on the second floor I was surprised to see the top of an ailanthus tree with young leaves just beginning to unfurl. Who had planted it and how its stubborn roots had ever managed to wring sustenance from the sour earth of that neglected back yard I have no idea, but I was grateful for finding even one thing in Potter's Alley that was not ugly.

I made a quick list of things I would have to get before dark: cot, blanket, can opener, cutlery. I must keep things down to the barest necessities to avoid any appearance of affluence that would make me conspicuous. That meant getting everything second-hand and going to more than one shop.

The electricity wasn't working. I could manage without cooking if I ate canned meats and vegetables, but I would have to have light. Candles and lanterns, perhaps. Dare I risk a portable television that worked on batteries? It was important for me to keep up with the latest news.

The man who was mending a broken window glanced at me covertly as I came out of the house. As soon as he saw that I had noticed his glance, his eyes fled in the other direction. Though I was as roughly dressed and unshaven as he, I was still a stranger and strangers were not trusted here.

I stopped at the delicatessen on the corner and said I would like to rent the second-floor back at 123. The man behind the counter was old and bald and bland. He wanted a hundred dollars, fifty for one month's rent and fifty for a deposit. I gave him a fifty-dollar bill and told him it was that or nothing. He pounced on it so predaciously I was sorry I hadn't offered him less.

"Do I get a key from you?" I asked him.

"Key?" He laughed. "There ain't no key. It ain't that kind of house."

Mentally I added a lock and key to my shopping list. Aloud I said: "Been empty quite a while, hasn't it?"

"Yeh." The bland smile faded. "Times are bad. More people moving out than moving in."

I wondered where they were moving to and then I remembered tales of the thirties. They would be moving in with parents or grandparents who doubtless lived in similar places. An independent home in Potter's Alley, however cramped, was becoming a luxury to many people.

A tall thin boy was lounging in the doorway when I came out of the delicatessen. He was dressed in slacks and shirt in two shades of turquoise. There was Indian jewelry, turquoise and silver, at his neck and wrists. He gave me the first grin I had encountered in Potter's Alley, but it was a prurient grin.

"Old Pete'll never tell you why that house has been empty so long."

"But you will?"

"Why not? Few years ago a fellow got high on mixing wine with pills and knifed a woman. One of those guys who likes to cut. Other folks moved out. Nobody else moved in."

I was right about it being a prurient grin. This was a story he relished in the telling.

"Then I won't be having neighbors inside the building?" I said.

"Maybe they'll start moving back once you're there." He looked me up and down speculatively. For the first time he was seeing me as a business opportunity. "You are moving in?"

"Yes, this afternoon."

"Anything you want let me know. I can get you lots of things."

"Things" meant girls, boys, hash or heroin. Cocaine was still for the carriage trade uptown.

76

"And where do I find you?" I asked.

He was too cagey to be precise about that. "Oh, I'll be around."

I watched him saunter away until he turned the corner. He was probably at the lowest level of the caste system in that criminal organization we used to call "The Family," too low to be of any use to me now.

I was much more interested in finding out who was following me and why.

I took the subway uptown and changed trains at 14th Street. When I finally got off at 42nd Street, I spotted him.

He was quite good. To an untrained eye he would have been invisible. Even I would have been hard put to it to describe him if asked to do so. Everything about him looked young except his hat, but it was functional, part of his camouflage, the oldest and simplest of all disguises: hat brim turned down and coat collar turned up to make the face invisible at a little distance.

I thought of brushing him off but then decided it would be more instructive to let him stay with me and see how he reacted when he saw the place where I was going. Most people would not recognize it, but I had a feeling he would.

I started walking east on 49th Street. As we passed big plate-glass windows that reflected the street I could see him trudging in my wake without turning my head. He was beginning to look a little tired.

The United Nations neighborhood has changed a lot in the last fifteen years. I could remember it when there were still some decent old bars and friendly, unpretentious restaurants. Now they were all swept away by what is called progress as if they had never been. In their place were highrises with vast walls of glass and small paved forecourts with tiny evergreens in wooden tubs like stage symbols of the gardens that weren't there.

The building where I was going was a little older than some of the others. It even had a directory of offices on the wall where company names still began with capital letters. I walked past this without looking at it and a guard stopped me.

"You know what floor you're going to?"

I could hardly blame him for stopping me. I must look pretty scruffy with my Potter's Alley clothes and a beard that had just reached the bristly stage.

"Top floor," I said.

"Oh . . ." I was interested to see the hostility that leapt into his eyes. He did not like the people on the top floor. At the same time he didn't dare stop anyone who was going there.

"There's a separate elevator for the penthouse," he said. "Last one in this row."

I pushed the only button. The elevator took off smoothly and silently. It was a whole minute before it came to a stop and I would not have known it had stopped if the doors had not glided apart.

In the lobby one wall was all glass doors leading to a roof terrace bathed in the brilliant sunshine that never reached the lower floors hemmed in by other buildings around them. I had seen the same effect in rain forests striated like the floors of a skyscraper with a few lucky bird species in the sunshine at the top and small mammals and reptiles in the twilight at root level.

At the reception desk there was no sign of the usual pied and sprightly girl exuding Aphrodisia or My Sin, but in her place a gnarled old gnome who looked exactly what he was, a retired sergeant of infantry named Murphy.

My appearance stunned him. It was the only time I had ever seen him at a loss for words. After a moment, he barked out without any preliminaries: "You gotta appointment?"

"Just tell Colonel Stebbins that I'm here."

"What name are you using now?"

Murphy could be tiresome about this sort of thing.

"Tell him that Samuel Joel is here. He'll know who it is."

78

I put a little iron in my voice. You couldn't be polite to Murphy. He thought politeness a weakness.

I couldn't hear what he growled into the voice box. He was keeping his voice low. After a moment he looked up and waved a hand towards the terrace.

"The Colonel will see you out there."

I went out through the glass door. There were tiles underfoot and a few deck chairs scattered about. It looked like the kind of place where secretaries ate sandwiches for luncheon. The view was magnificent. You could look over rooftops to both rivers and Jersey and Brooklyn beyond.

I heard a step behind me and turned around.

"George—"

"I'm Sam now. Sam Joel."

"Whoever you are, you have no business here. For your own sake, you're not supposed to get in touch with the Agency at any time for any reason."

"I'm not getting in touch with the Agency. I'm seeing an old friend, Timothy Stebbins, who believe it or not, is now a full colonel."

He laughed and looked more like the old Steb I used to know. He is a small man, but wiry and tough and shrewd. He can be kind, too, whenever the Agency allows him to be himself.

"That's a questionable distinction. Don't tell me what you're doing now. I don't want to know. Just tell me what you want."

"First of all, I want to know who's following me. One of yours?"

"I doubt it, but I'll check. Why would we be following you?"

"So you still don't read the papers here at the Agency?"

He blinked. "You're in the news?"

"Come on, Steb. Even you must have read about the Endicott kidnapping."

"You're involved in that?"

"Samuel Joel is involved. Didn't you notice the name?"

"No." He could have been lying for devious Agency reasons, but I didn't think he was. More likely a new press secretary had not thought it important enough to include my name in summaries of spot news for him.

"How are you involved?"

"I was there when it happened."

"Did you know the Endicotts in Vietnam?"

"No, only in Connecticut where we've both been living."

"I still don't see why we should be following you. We're not interested in this case."

"But I'm in the case," I retorted. "Somebody here might retain a little interest in me."

"I doubt that, but I'll check on it now."

He went back into the lobby. Through the glass door I saw him pick up a telephone on Murphy's desk. He came back after a few moments.

"They say not."

"Can I believe that?"

He smiled. "You know how we are here. The left hand never knows what the right hand is doing and neither of them have the remotest idea what the feet are up to. Let's just say it is probably true. Who else might have a reason for following you?"

I thought about that for a moment. Digby might have sent a man to see what I was up to when I left Connecticut. It was barely possible that the Hashashin might have noticed me in Lamborn Street and were now making sure that I didn't get too close to wherever they were hiding Kate.

Far more likely than either of these possibilities was The Family. I had expected them to show an interest in me the moment I took that money out of the bank. The circulation of money is something that it is almost impossible to keep secret. Too many people have routine access to that sort of information.

"Well?" said Steb.

I told him what I was thinking.

He looked unhappy. "You do understand there's nothing we can do to protect you?" he said.

"You made that very clear when you got rid of me," I retorted. "I don't want your protection. All I want from you is a little information."

"What kind of information?"

"Kate's mother was a Vietnamese. She and Adam Endicott were divorced ten years ago, and she married a Frenchman, Ghislain de Boisron."

"And sometimes parents who lose custody of a child resort to kidnapping?"

"It's rare but it does happen, even years after a divorce. It's the one form of kidnapping where the law never invokes the death penalty. I want to know where she is now. Can you find out?"

"I can try. Wait a minute."

This time he was gone much longer. Everything was taking longer than I had thought it would.

Even the view began to pall and once more I longed for the cigarettes I had promised myself I would never smoke again.

I walked up and down the terrace until I was sick of it. I had just flopped in one of the deck chairs when Steb came back.

"You're in luck," he said. "I was afraid you'd have to go to Paris or the Far East, but she's living in New York."

"Did you get the address?"

He handed me a page torn from a memorandum pad.

Ed Robbins, 26 Jefferson Place, Brooklyn.

"Is she married for a second time?"

"I don't know. Robbins works for *The New York Times.*"

"Anything else about her?"

81

"Her first name is Precious Jade."

I put the paper in my pocket. "Thanks, Steb."

I turned to go, but he put a hand on my arm. "George, have you spent any of that money we gave you?"

"Yes."

"How much?"

"Fifty thousand."

"All at once? Why?"

"Adam Endicott couldn't raise enough cash in time to pay the ransom money when they wanted it."

"So you are involved with this girl."

"I'm trying to find her while she's still alive, if that's what you mean."

"You think you can do what the FBI and the Connecticut State Police have failed to do so far?"

"I can try. There are some advantages in being an individual. Fewer rules and regulations."

"Has it occurred to you that the whole thing may be a put-up job? That Katherine Endicott may have connived at her own kidnapping from the beginning?"

"You're asking me to believe that Kate joined a conspiracy to extort money from her own father by exploiting his anxiety about her safety and freedom? I'll believe that when Kate tells me so herself, but not before."

"Now wait a minute, George—"

But I was too angry to say goodbye. I just got out of there as fast as I could.

9

I broke my own rule and took a taxi to Brooklyn. I thought I was far enough from Lamborn Street to risk it. It might be quicker than the rush hour on the subway, and it certainly would be more comfortable. So far as I could tell no one was following the taxi.

The best view of downtown Manhattan in the city is from Brooklyn Bridge at that hour of the evening when the sun has just set. I don't really like vertical architecture, skyscrapers and Gothic cathedrals. Both would have appalled the ancient Greeks, but I forget all that when I see those brilliantly lit towers growing brighter every moment against a sky growing darker every moment.

When I was a small boy, my mother used to compare those towers at dusk to giant honeycombs and their serried windows to cells, loaded and dripping with rich, golden, luminous honey. Tonight I saw them quite differently as galaxies at the farthest edge of the universe, useless beacons shining across an infinite wasteland that we could neither traverse nor understand.

I knew what that meant. The isolation in which I was living now was beginning to prey on my mind.

We plunged into the narrow streets around Borough Hall

and the splendor of the view vanished as if it had been a mirage.

I had a Manhattan driver and I had not been on Brooklyn Heights since I trudged to the old Friends' primary school on Schermerhorn Street, so we had to question passersby and watch street signs and stop to peer at house numbers in shadowy, recessed doorways before we found Jefferson Place.

Number 26 was a large old town house, still standing in about two acres of priceless New York real estate. There was a coach house in the back, probably a garage today, but you could still recognize double doors to stabling on the ground floor and a row of windows upstairs that suggested an apartment for the coachman and his family. It wasn't really so long ago as it sounds. In my mother's childhood there were more hansom cabs on Fifth Avenue than what were then called motor cars.

The taxi driver lit another match and we discovered that the Number was 24. The coach house was Number 26, my destination.

It was already night under the tall trees in that cobblestoned yard where the coach house stood. Next to its double doors was a smaller door, possibly once the door to a tackroom. There were lights in the windows on the upper floor.

"Shall I wait?" asked the taxi driver.

I said: "No, thanks," paid him off and rang the bell.

The door was opened by a man who was probably older than he looked. It was the unruly mop of dark hair that made him look young. There were a good many years of experience in his alert, intelligent face. He was dressed like a Wall Street banker, waistcoat, white shirt, dark tie, discreetly polished shoes.

I had actually forgotten how I was dressed until I saw his eyes narrow impatiently as he looked at me.

"Yes?" he said curtly. "What do you want?"

"I'm looking for Ed Robbins," I said. "It's about Katherine Endicott."

"Oh . . ." His manner changed. It was not more friendly, but it was more tolerant. "Will you please come upstairs?"

The stairway was steep and narrow. He was a man with the habit of courage for he turned his back on me and went up first. I am not at all sure that I would have done that myself in today's New York with a stranger who looked as I looked. Some people are temperamentally incapable of caution in any environment. I wondered if he was one of them.

He opened a door and stood back to let me enter a living-room so large it looked like an old hayloft remodelled. There were windows at either end now and a modern Chinese rug that used the old symbols of peace and longevity in soft colors, cream and sand and muted green. Every color in the room was in the same key and octave. There was no dissonance, no jolt for the eye anywhere.

It was an ideal setting for the exquisite little person who sat on a deep silken sofa beside the warm, bright fire on the hearth.

She had Kate's delicate profile, ivory skin and sleek black hair, but, unlike Kate, the Mongol fold was clearly marked in the upper eyelids, giving her eyes that half-closed, sleepy look that is so fascinating once you are used to it.

She wore the *ao dai* of Vietnam. The word means "long dress" and of all Asiatic costumes it is the most graceful because of its mobility. It drifts and floats with every movement of the wearer and every current of air as if it were made of mist or smoke or flame. This was made of the lightest and softest of all silks, the Chinese "palace silk," and it was the creamy color of a pearl.

My appearance startled her, and her eyes flew to the man beside me. *"Ghislain, qu'est-ce . . . ?"*

"Il s'agit de Kate."

"Ghislain?" I said. "Not Ed Robbins?"

He smiled. "A pen-name and partly an anagram. " 'Ed' is 'de' in reverse. If you drop the extra 'O' in 'Boisron' and add an extra 'B,' the letters can be used to spell 'Robbins.' Ghislain de Boisron is too exotic for the stories I write. They do better if the readers think I'm Ed Robbins, one of the boys."

I had never heard a Frenchman speak English so totally without a French intonation and I remarked on this.

"I was one of the French children sent here to escape the bombing after France fell in 1940."

"Perhaps it would have been better for him if he had stayed in France," said Precious Jade. "Now he will always be halfway between two cultures, never quite French and never quite American, just as I am never quite French and never quite Vietnamese."

"Is that so bad?" I said. "I spent years of my youth in Southeast Asia and I am sure I live halfway between two cultures, but isn't that what the world needs today, people who are at home in at least two countries?"

"Possibly." She smiled and it was Kate's "archaic smile." "Do sit down. As you have probably guessed, I am Kate's mother. Tell us about Kate." There was a shiver in her voice, slight as the trembling of a shadow. "You have news of her? You wish to earn the reward?"

"I didn't even know there was a reward."

"We are offering ten thousand dollars. It is in the evening papers."

"I haven't seen the evening papers and I don't want a reward. I want to find Kate and I need your help. My name is Samuel Joel."

Ghislain recognized that name instantly. Unlike the man in the Agency, newspaper men read newspapers instead of having spot news summarized by a secretary.

"You're the man who was shot trying to save Kate," he said.

"I'd better tell you the whole story," I answered.

So that was how I came to tell them all the things the newspapers didn't know or didn't think worth printing.

I didn't have to tell them I loved Kate. They could see that and I saw no reason for holding back anything about myself. Indeed I wanted Kate's mother and stepfather to know everything about me there was to know.

It was the first time in many years that I had talked so frankly to anyone and I enjoyed the emotional luxury of honest confession, something I had rarely experienced.

"It takes an organization to get information of the kind we need," I told them. "I never could have found you so quickly if I hadn't gone to an organization, the Agency, for your address, but they have no idea where Kate is now, or so they say. Neither apparently do the FBI or the Connecticut State Police. If any of them knew where she was, she would have been arrested. What we need now is someone who has contact with organizations in the criminal underworld."

This amused Ghislain. "You think I have that?"

"Not personally, but an active newspaper man has many sources of information that most people don't have, especially in his own city. You know the police here. Through them you must know some police informers. You hear gossip at every social level. How else would you ever get an idea for a story? You've been a staff correspondent. Now you have more freedom as an independent freelance writing successful feature stories."

"You've been looking at back files of my paper."

"Of course. The New Hashashin are here in New York and New York is your town. You've a better chance of finding out where they are keeping Kate than anyone else."

"You think I haven't tried?"

"I'm sure you have, but you had no guidelines. It must have been like closing your eyes and sticking a pin in a map. Now you know that the Hashashin are probably in that part of the East Village near Lamborn Street where I'm holed up."

"Then you came to me primarily because I am a newspaper man?"

"I came to you primarily because you are Kate's stepfather."

Ghislain looked at his wife. He must have read an answer in her eyes for he turned back to me briskly. *"Bon!* You can count on me."

Precious Jade let her breath go in a long sigh as if she had been holding it for some time. "You do understand, Mr. Joel, that I love my daughter?"

"Naturally."

"No, not naturally. Many people think I do not love her, because I left Adam when leaving him meant losing Kate. At the time I thought it best for her. Now I'm not so sure. Now I know that losing a child for any reason is the wound that never heals."

"You are not doing yourself justice, Jade." Ghislain pronounced her name with a broad French "A" and a soft French "J." The word sounded gentler than it does in English.

He turned back to me. "Adam was obsessively jealous. He couldn't be with Jade without quarrelling with her even when Kate, a child, was present."

"That doesn't sound like the Adam I knew."

"Did you ever really know him?"

Did I?

I had always admired Adam for marrying outside his own race and culture, but now an unwelcome thought intruded: Had the marriage broken down because of the difference in race and culture?

Adam's generation had prejudices my generation did not understand. Perhaps he had inherited prejudices that he didn't want to admit to himself. A marriage founded on such self-deception would be flawed from the beginning. The lightest tap would split it, as a diamond splits, along the line of the flaw.

I even began to wonder if Adam's sudden hostility to me when he suspected that I loved Kate was rooted in possessive jealousy rather than concern for her.

Was I ever going to feel quite the same about Adam again? Precious Jade read the thought in my eyes.

"Men are different at different periods of their lives," she said. "And they are even more different when they are with different people. Your Adam and my Adam were not the same man. Try to forget mine and keep yours as you remember him."

But I knew I couldn't, not now.

"I would like to see that gold chain with the carnelian bead," went on Jade. "Did you leave it in Connecticut?"

"No." I took it out of my pocket.

She turned it over in her hands gently, lovingly. "Yes, it is Kate's. I gave it to her when she was two years old."

Ghislain had been lost in thought for a moment. Now he looked at both of us.

"Do you know the old Charleston story of Madame Margot? In extremity she prayed to God for help and there was no answer. Then came a lightning flash and a thunder crash and a sardonic voice said: 'Why not try me?'

"It was, of course, the voice of the Devil.

"We are in a somewhat similar situation. God, that is, the powers that be, are not helping us. Why don't we try the Devil, that is, The Family? Any objections?"

"You mean Enzo?" said Jade.

"Of course. Who else do I know who has any connections with The Family?"

"I am afraid this isn't going to work," I said.

"Why?" demanded Ghislain.

"The Family do not like me. I think they are having me followed and I know they would never do anything to help me in any situation."

"Is there a particular reason for this hostility?" asked Jade.

I saw then that I would have to tell them the whole story. Strangely I felt it was going to be a relief to talk frankly. It was

89

a long time since I had been perfectly frank with anyone.

"Everything that people believe about me now is untrue," I said. "My name is not Samuel Joel. I was not born in China. I did not go to college in Middlebury and I was never employed by the *Washington Post* when I was in Vietnam."

"Then Samuel Joel is a myth?"

"No, he was a real person. He did all the things I am supposed to have done and then died in an air raid. He had no close, surviving relatives. Neither did I. I didn't even have close friends at home because I had spent most of my life abroad.

"So there was nothing to keep the Agency from endowing me with his past and his passport. I don't look much like him, but that hardly mattered as long as I buried myself alive in Greenwood where no one who had known him was likely to run into me."

"What is your real name?"

"George Hardy."

"What happened to him?"

"He is dead on paper. Samuel Joel was buried under his name."

"Everybody has heard of these Agency tricks," said Ghislain. "But aren't they used only when a man's own identity will endanger his life?"

"They said mine would."

"What had you done?"

I looked down at the Chinese rug with its ancient symbols of peace and longevity. That was easier than watching their faces.

"I was brought up in Japan during the occupation. My father was a soldier *manqué*. He came from one of those old Army families that sends a son to West Point in each generation but he was born color blind, so West Point wouldn't accept him as officer material when he was a boy. Even after Pearl Harbor he could only get a job as a civilian employee of the Army. He hated that. He had romantic illusions about military life.

"Eventually he became the editor of an English-language newspaper published in Tokyo. As I was born in 1944, I was just the right age when Vietnam came along. With a father like mine and an upbringing like mine, it was inevitable that I should volunteer. Imagine volunteering for the first war in history to become a tourist attraction to the jet set, and a TV show for the folks back home.

"I often felt like that French Colonel who looked around at the dead and dying in 1870 and cried out: 'How stupid!' "

"I know that story." Ghislain smiled. "It was Colonel de Rochas and his actual words were: *'Que c'est bête!'* "

"In the beginning I was detailed to the Agency because of languages. I didn't see the rough side of the war until I was made a prisoner during the Tet offensive, and sent to the 'Hanoi Hilton,' the old municipal prison in the center of Hanoi.

"I did not make a good prisoner. I discovered that I am temperamentally resistant to coercion and even persuasion if it is too aggressive. The fact that I hated the war and sympathized with so many of the Vietnamese made me all the more resistant. It would have been so easy for me to rationalize a defection, but if you are going to defect it must be an act of free will or it is nothing. I had to resist that temptation. There was only one way to do it—escape—so that is what I did."

"That must have been quite a feat. I'd like to hear the details."

"I doubt if you would. It's not a pleasant story.

"I was younger then and pretty naïve. It never occurred to me that the Agency might suspect that I had been allowed to escape by my captors so that I could become a double agent."

Jade caught her breath but Ghislain said calmly enough: "Did they suspect that?"

"I'll never be quite sure, but I think it is the reason they gave me such a dangerous assignment when I went on active duty again. I suppose you may have heard that some members of The Family collaborated discreetly with the local black market to supply troops with heroin and other hard drugs. I was assigned to infiltrate that operation as an undercover agent. Anyone discovered by The Family infiltrating their drug setup does not live long once his cover is exposed. Mine was exposed early in the game and I never found out just how it happened."

"Ingenious," said Ghislain. "Instead of risking your acquittal by a general court martial, they simply blew your cover to The Family? If The Family couldn't, or wouldn't, dispose of you, they themselves could still use the Family threat to force you to bury yourself alive, where you couldn't do any more harm?"

"Put so bluntly it does sound like a classic case of paranoia," I admitted. "After all, the transfer of identity was a smooth, professional job and they were quite generous with severance pay, though they did warn me that it would be risky to spend the money all at once in the next ten years. Any appearance of sudden affluence on my part might draw the attention of The Family to me with disagreeable consequences."

"You can forget that if you decide to go with me to Enzo's," said Ghislain. "He's even more of a maverick than you are. He's a reluctant Mafioso. He's probably the only man who ever defied The Family and got away without disagreeable consequences. After all, The Family's power is based on quick, merciless punishment for spies and traitors."

"Oh, Ghislain!" cried Jade. "After all Sam has told us, do you still think it wise to take him to see Enzo?"

"Not wise perhaps, my dear," said Ghislain. "But necessary. Who else can help us find Kate?"

"Tell me more about Enzo," I said.

"His name is Lorenzo Visconti," said Ghislain. "But he is no relation of the ducal family. He was born at the end of the

Second World War when The Family had amassed such enormous war profits that they began looking around for respectable investments instead of just plowing the profits back into the old, traditional Family business of vice, extortion and murder.

"Enzo's father was killed when he was a baby. His mother remained a widow. Like many women in The Family, she had only a vague idea of what was going on. She knew there were some technical illegalities, but according to Enzo himself she did not know that crime was involved and so neither did he when he was a growing boy. The Family always takes care of its own for this is an important source of power in any society, so she was able to live well in a New Jersey suburb and send Enzo to all the best schools and colleges.

"He grew up innocent. The elder generation of males running The Family were not close relatives of his and they didn't realize what was happening to him. You may imagine the shock to them and to Enzo himself when they told him the truth and offered him a Family career as they had always intended to do when he came of age.

"With his upbringing and their dedication to business it was a moment of acute embarrassment for all of them.

"Contrary to popular belief, The Family has been pulling away from illegality for some time. They now actually try to avoid unnecessary hits because such incidents are bad public relations and the deeper their investment in respectable business, the more they want to avoid a bad press.

"The dispute between Enzo and the others went on for a day or so. Enzo's moral position was weakened by the fact that he had grown up in great affluence and didn't wish to give up his income, but The Family argued that if he wished to retain his income, he must earn it as they earned theirs.

"It was his mother who suggested the final compromise, If The Family would spare Enzo all involvement in the business, they could make his income contingent on his silence about them and everything they did. If he broke that silence, his life would be forfeit.

"This has now been going on for several years and Enzo is unhappy. Like most of us, he wants to eat his cake and have it. He has the conscience of a weak man. It needles him night and day but never hard enough to affect his conduct.

"So now he has worked out his own little compromise with his own conscience, a sort of secret codicil to his compromise with The Family. He makes a clandestine practice of leaking information to a few newspaper men like me. It's not half as dangerous as it sounds. The leads are distributed among so many newspapers that they cannot be traced to any one source and therefore eventually to Enzo. The information actually published is chosen carefully so that a dozen other people besides Enzo might have leaked it. We are never seen in public with him, only in his own home where his own technicians have taken every precaution against electronic eavesdropping. So far he has got away with it for several years, but . . .

"We all know what happens to the pitcher that goes to the well too often. One of these days we'll pick up the morning paper and see that Enzo has disappeared. That will be the end of it and all of us who let him feed us information are going to feel a little guilty.

"Most of Enzo's customers rather despise the poor little tick, the way cops despise stool pigeons, but I rather like him. Sometimes I wonder how many of us would have acted differently in his situation? I can understand his not wanting to give up the income he's used to and I can also understand his wanting to hit back secretly at the people who destroyed his illusions. I don't say I would have done it myself, but it's quite human."

"In other words, Ghislain has been using Enzo as little as possible because of the risk to Enzo," said Jade. "But this one time he will have to be used again."

94

"The sooner the better," I said. "Tonight?"

She looked at a French carriage clock on the mantelpiece, old enough to have come from Breguet's workshop in its heyday.

"I think there's time. He always stays up late."

"Perhaps I should telephone first." Ghislain went out of the room.

"It's getting colder," said Jade. "You should both have cognac before you go."

She took two glasses from a cupboard and filled them from a decanter. "The French are now trying to prove that people who drink cognac live longer than everybody else."

I laughed.

"It's not a joke. It's a theory."

"The French are very enterprising in matters of trade. What's the theory?"

"They claim there is some kind of mold in cognac that kills germs, just like penicillin. Of course you must not drink too much cognac, but then neither must you eat too much penicillin."

Again I had that unpleasant feeling of being divided. One half of me might sit here and laugh about the medicinal value of cognac. The other half of me was far away in a trance of anxiety about Kate. Was Precious Jade divided, too, and going through the motions of normal life without the feelings?

Ghislain came back with a new briskness in his manner.

"All settled. We have a rendezvous an hour from now. That allows thirty minutes to get there and thirty minutes to find a parking place, which is just about right."

"Allow two minutes for this." Jade handed him the other glass of cognac.

"You are not supposed to toss down good cognac like beer," protested Ghislain. "You are supposed to savor it. However, just this once . . ." He tossed it down.

"Promise me this is the last time you will see Enzo?" said

Jade, and I knew she was not thinking about the risk to Enzo then.

Ghislain smiled. "I promise, if that will make you happy."

He put his fingertips under her chin and lifted it gently so their lips met for a moment.

You can always tell in the way a man and a woman behave to each other whether they are happy together or not. These two were happy. I was glad Kate's mother had found happiness in this marriage no matter what had gone wrong with her marriage to Adam.

Down in the courtyard we found something between rain and the mist from the harbor that you get so often on Brooklyn Heights.

"Perhaps it would be wiser not to take my car," said Ghislain. "It's too easily recognized. Why don't we walk to the subway and pick up a cab in Manhattan?"

No one else was walking in the rain on that street at that hour. Our footfalls were in step ringing clear on the asphalt with now and then something like an echo.

I began telling Ghislain how the old Brooklynites had objected when their city was made a mere borough of New York.

As he made no response, I fell silent, reminding myself that other people's family memories are as boring as other people's dreams.

In this I did him an injustice.

After a moment or two of silence, he said quietly: "I think we are being followed."

10

It was in the subway that I finally got a good look at him. He was shabbily dressed, but not so shabby as to be conspicuous. Just a general crumpling, fraying and abrasion of clothes that suggested a man playing a losing game with life, wearing out things that he could not afford to repair or replace.

We still couldn't see his face. Between the hat brim and the coat collar there was only a gleam of eyes in shadow. But I was pretty sure he was young. His gait, his bearing, everything were those of a boy rather than a man.

I pointed him out to Ghislain.

"Perhaps we should ask your friend Enzo if he is from The Family?"

"He looks too young for that," said Ghislain, confirming my own impression.

We changed trains at 14th Street in Manhattan, but our friend managed to stay with us. He was more professional than he looked.

"We'll have to shake him before we keep our appointment," said Ghislain. "Enzo's double life is quite complicated enough without our leading an unknown quantity to his door. Have you any idea who this is?"

I shook my head. "The Agency does not as a rule employ

amateurs and this man is an amateur. Otherwise we would not have noticed him. He looks like one of those who infiltrate the anticulture and sell information to anyone who wants it. They're not on anybody's staff. They get paid according to each bit of information they bring in."

"That's more like it," said Ghislain. "A freelance who might be working for anybody. But why the interest in us?"

"It's probably an interest in me," I said. "Someone was following me yesterday, but I had no idea who he was or what he was after. I thought I had shaken him when I came to your house."

"We'll have to shake this one now before we get anywhere near Enzo's. Any suggestions?"

"I'm afraid it's up to you. I haven't been in New York since I was a boy and everything has changed."

"All right then, we'll play follow-the-leader and I'll be the leader. We'll move to the middle door now and get off at the next stop but one."

We stood by the door in the middle of the train as it opened and closed again. There was a little knot of standees behind us and our shadow. How well the word suited him! You rarely heard a sound from him, but if you glanced backward quickly you were likely to catch a silent flicker of movement gone the next second.

The train slowed to a stop and the door opened again. It had started to close once more when Ghislain said softly: "Now!" and pushed through. I followed, close behind him, and the door slammed behind me.

Ghislain did not run on the platform or even quicken his pace. The man behind us might be watching us from a window as the train pulled out. Better leave him uncertain whether we were aware of his pursuit or not.

But when we left the platform for the stairs, Ghislain took them two steps at a time.

We came out in the basement of a large office building and

sped up another stair to its ground floor. Shops there were closed and dark at this hour, but there were a few lights in the lobby near the front entrance and one elevator despatcher on duty for the sake of night visitors.

Ghislain turned in the other direction and opened a door leading by way of a long, connecting corridor into another building. Here again there were comparatively few lights in the lobby and only one man on duty. He was standing beside a lectern with a register for the signatures of everyone who entered the building after hours. He looked at us with sudden curiosity.

"I didn't see you come in, did I?"

Ghislain smiled brilliantly. "But now you're going to see us go out!"

Before the man could recover we were in the street.

By going through those two big buildings we had traversed a whole city block from one east-west side street to another, but Ghislain was not through manoeuvring yet. The second side street was choked with a traffic jam at that moment. They looked like people bound for theaters and night clubs. He slid like an eel through stalled cars and I followed.

We came out on a sidewalk in front of a small bar, all Musak and neon lights. Inside we had to push our way through a crowd of standees waiting for orders around the bar, muttering a ritual "excuse-me-sorry-beg-pardon" as we shouldered bodies aside and tried not to step on toes without attracting too much attention.

We came up for air in a dining-space where only a dozen or so tables were grouped around a tiny dance floor and edged our way around the dancers to the other side of the room.

Here someone had been lewdly coy about labelling one door COCKS and the other HENS.

Without hesitation, Ghislain plunged through the one marked HENS.

"No one would think of looking for us here," he said blithely.

A corridor ran past the swing door to another door that led to an alley. It was locked but the key was in the lock on this side. He turned it and we walked out. At the mouth of the alley, a taxi was just passing. He hailed it and said: "Drive through the Park."

We were both panting a little as we settled into the back seat.

"It certainly is useful to have someone along who knows the town," I said.

"Yes, isn't it?" But his quick smile faded as we both turned our heads to look out the rear window.

After a few moments Ghislain said: "He's gone . . ." Only then did he give the driver an address on Central Park South.

"You know," he went on to me. "The most important things in these situations are speed and surprise. What you do quickly, and unexpectedly, no one can catch up with. A thing done suddenly leaves no time for adequate response."

He was watching the rear-view mirror now. "No car behind us," he reported. "And no single man on the pavement. Just one old woman. Nonetheless I think we'll leave this cab here and walk the last few blocks to Enzo's."

The drizzle was gone. Walking through the rain-washed air was refreshing. We came to one of the smaller apartment houses between Fifth and Sixth and Ghislain turned into the lobby.

He spoke to a man there as if this were a first visit.

"Mrs. Monroe's floor?"

"Sixteenth, sir. Whom shall I announce?"

"Just say Ed Robbins."

I saw the advantage of the pen-name now. If he had said Ghislain de Boisron he would have had to spell it out and the man would have remembered it.

100

The response that came out of the voice box was an unintelligble squawk to me but our man must have understood it for he signalled to another man who took us to an elevator and entered with us.

In besieged New York people who can afford top prices for apartments want no part of unmanned elevators, the mugger's delight.

I could remember when you used to step directly from an elevator into the charming hallway of an apartment occupying a whole floor. Tonight we stepped into a small vestibule where we were confronted by a door secured by two locks and a peephole fitted with one-way glass. Only after we had been scrutinized was the door opened.

The man who held the door open looked to me like one of those Sicilians of Saracen descent who still look more Arab than Italian. He ushered us through a vast, shadowy living-room where only one lamp was burning and onto a terrace that covered the whole roof of the building.

After all I had heard about Enzo I looked at him with considerable interest. He looked to me like one of the Sicilians of Greek descent who still have the harmony of feature that makes Hellenic sculpture so pleasant to look upon. Unfortunately, as in most Hellenic sculpture that has survived, there were signs of erosion.

The splendid lines of fine bone structure were beginning to blur under a film of fat. He was probably spending too much time as he was now, lounging in a long chair with a book in one hand, a cigarette in the other and a decanter on the table beside him. There would be sweet sherry or Marsala or Madeira in the decanter. I could see that the plate, even closer to his hand on the table, was loaded with all sorts of deadly and delicious forms of cholesterol: *chocolats, liqueurs,* purée of chestnuts with whipped cream and wine-frosted grapes.

A reluctant Mafioso who lets himself run to fat before he is thirty is obviously not a happy young man.

He was pleased to see Ghislain. He looked at me more warily. I remembered what Ghislain had said about the values of speed and surprise, so I plunged into the middle of things.

"You should know the truth about me," I said. "The Family does not like me."

"Why?"

Ghislain intervened.

"Sam was with the Agency in Vietnam. There was a little disagreement about providing troops with heroin."

"Just the sort of stupid, unnecessary thing they would do," remarked Enzo. "Are they bothering you about it now?"

"Someone has been shadowing him," said Ghislain.

"You have my sympathy, but what can I do?" Enzo shrugged elaborately, using his hands and elbows as well as his shoulders. "My only connection with The Family now is the money I get from them. We have agreed to disagree. So long as I leave them alone, they leave me alone."

He reached for a brandied cherry. "Do help yourselves." He chewed noisily. "If you don't like wine, there's Scotch and other barbarous drinks over there in the cabinet."

His gaze came back to me. "If The Family thought for one moment that I was working against them, I'd be in worse trouble than you."

"You won't be working against them," said Ghislain. "All we want from you is a little information about Katherine Endicott."

"Why do you care about her?"

"Didn't you know she is my wife's daughter?"

"No, I didn't know." Enzo sat up and turned in his chair so he could bring his feet to the floor. His eyes were sympathetic now. "The Family had nothing to do with that kidnapping."

"I know," said Ghislain. "It's an amateur's crime."

"So why come to me?"

"Because The Family has the best intelligence network in

102

the underground. We want to know who is holding Kate and where, and we're in a hurry. The longer she's held, the greater the danger."

"I see." Enzo sighed windily. "Ghislain, if it were any other crime in the world, I wouldn't lift a finger to help you, but I can't refuse to help with this one. I can't promise results, but let's see what I can do. I'll make a few telephone calls."

"Is that safe?" asked Ghislain.

"My private lines are safer than the hot line from Washington to Moscow," said Enzo. "If you don't like the drinks on the table, do try the cabinet."

But neither Ghislain nor I felt like drinking now. Drinks are for relaxation. We wanted to stay wound up taut and alert tonight.

It seemed a long time before Enzo came back, and when he did he was frowning.

"It's not much," he said. "But it's something. The name and address of a loft building in the wasteland below Canal Street."

He handed me a slip of paper. My brain took in the meaning of the written words slowly. They were not at all what I had expected. They seemed absurd.

Moon Mother, 271 Beekman Street. No telephone.

"Who is this supposed to be?" I asked.

"A woman who was with the kidnappers when they were at the old Delano place in Greenwood. No one seems to know any other name for her than Moon Mother. Perhaps she doesn't have one. There's a boy with her, a son or grandson, who seems to be suffering from some kind of brain damage."

"This looks as if it might be what I've been hoping for," I said. "The first real lead of any kind into the identity of the kidnappers. Until now they've just been phantom voices on tape recordings and you can't fight phantoms. You've put flesh on them. Now I can begin to think of them as real people. You can fight real people."

"I also had a chance to ask if anyone had been assigned to

shadow you," said Enzo. "My informant said: 'No,' but I'll keep after it. And now it's after midnight, and a long way to Brooklyn, so you'd better let me send you home in my car."

It was a limousine with soundproof, bulletproof glass between chauffeur and passengers. Ghislain was full of plans for tomorrow. Perhaps we should pass this tip on to the New York office of the FBI in the morning. They had not been involved in the case before and they might not share Digby's prejudice against Kate and all her generation and—

I stopped him.

"Ghislain, all we have is one name, undoubtedly fake, and one address, probably temporary. Whether Moon Mother is one of the kidnappers or not, Kate may not be with her at that address now."

"So?"

"If the FBI or the New York Police or any big organization goes crashing in they may frighten the birds away. This is an occasion for quiet, undercover observation."

"But there's so little time!"

"If Moon Mother is frightened away by a direct attack we'll be right back where we started, with nothing. Give me twenty-four hours to reconnoiter. That's all I ask."

"You alone?"

"Me alone. I can pass in the underground. You can't. You don't look or speak the part of a member of the anticulture. I can do both. I've already established a sort of identity in the East Village where you would stick out like an atomic bomb. I get by because I'm not altogether playing a part. After years of uprooting and exile I'm more at home in the underground than lots of other places."

He was disappointed, but I had an argument he couldn't ignore. At last he let me persuade him to drop me at the 57th Street subway station.

"You haven't even a telephone," he said. "How am I going

to reach you if something important comes up?"

"I have one friend left at the Agency, Colonel Stebbins. You could leave a message with him. He won't talk and I shall keep in touch with him."

I took a train to 14th Street and there consulted a map to find what train would take me nearest to Beekman Street. I had no intention of waiting until tomorrow morning before I began reconnoitering.

When I left the second train at Bowling Green, it was so late that I was alone on the platform. The train went roaring, clattering, shrieking and grinding on down the track and I walked towards the stairs, my footfalls loud in the sudden silence.

Harsh lights banished shadows here but the place was not one where I could feel comfortable. It would have made a congenial subject for one of those surrealistic painters who have the trick of making bright, empty space more menacing than darkness, as if there must be something horrible just beyond the light.

I suppose the emptiness suggests silence and loneliness and both are questions always asking us what lies beyond. That is why solitary confinement breaks down a prisoner.

My footfalls were loud in the silence. So was the creak of the turnstiles as I went through.

When I reached the top of the stairs and took my first steps into the street the air seemed deliciously fresh after the stale subway smells.

I paused a moment to get my bearings and then set off walking south.

It took me about ten minutes to find Beekman Street. It was a wide street for that part of town lined with loft buildings and warehouses. Most of them were dark, but here and there a scattering of lights identified a few lofts used as dwelling places because they were spacious and cheap.

The street numbers increased as I went and the odd numbers were on the other side of the street. So I had to cross over and walk south to find 271. As I approached it the neighborhood began to change a little. There were still loft buildings but there was also a few small shops now, a delicatessen, an electrical repair shop, a newspaper, candy and tobacco place, all obviously catering to the new people who now lived in the lofts.

Number 269 was a warehouse with a garage attached. The sliding, overhead door for cars was closed and presumably locked, but a smaller door, possibly for the use of a night watchman, was standing ajar.

An open door at that hour of the night seemed so odd that my pace slowed for a moment in sheer astonishment. Subconsciously I must have heard a movement behind me for I dodged just before a heavy blow aimed at my head landed painfully but relatively harmlessly against my shoulder.

Years ago I had various courses in American unarmed combat and Chinese "martial arts." They all tend to establish reflex responses to attack that bypass the thinking process when there is no time for it.

Someone was trying to break my wrist. I turned and kept on turning like a spinning top and he let go and went down with a scream. Someone else had hands at my throat but using only two fingers I threw up his arms and he staggered back. I didn't have a good look at either one, but I had an impression they were both young.

I slipped through the open doorway, slammed and bolted the door behind me. I was in a small cubicle where there was an armchair, a table and a half-eaten sandwich. Someone had just plugged in an electric tea kettle. Obviously a night watchman's place, but there was no sign of the watchman.

I saw another door and pushed it open.

I was at the bottom of an enclosed stairway with cinder-

106

block walls and concrete steps, a door and a light on each landing. Obviously a fire stair.

In my folly I decided that it would be a simple matter to run up a few flights, come down in an elevator and find an exit to another street.

I went up four flights and reached for the knob of the door on that landing only to find that it would not turn. The door was locked.

Then I remembered. In many buildings today it is the custom to lock fire-stair doors on the inside of each hallway. In the event of fire a janitor has to unlock all the doors, but this is considered less hazardous than leaving the doors unlocked so that anyone who breaks into a basement garage can walk up the fire stairs and reach any floor at any hour of the day or night.

By going up the fire stairs I had walked into a trap from which there was no exit at all.

Already I could hear blows on the flimsy door to the watchman's cubicle. In another moment I heard several feet running up the stairs towards me.

II

When I opened my eyes I was lying at the foot of the stairway on the street floor. Beyond the still open door I could see the watchman's cubicle in the dull light of a smoggy, city dawn.

Hands touched my face gently. A soft, slow voice said: "You hurt bad."

It was a voice I had heard twice before, once on a telephone and once on a tape recording.

I heard footfalls moving away and closed my eyes.

The next thing I remember is the coolness of a damp cloth touching sore spots on my face.

"Just cleaning up the dirt," said the voice. "You like a drink of water?"

I started to nod and thought better of it. "Yes."

An arm under my back raised me and a plastic cup was brought to my lips. The water made me realize I was thirsty. I drank and opened my eyes. I saw blood in the water.

I managed to speak again. "More."

I was sitting up now. After I drank the second cup of water I looked at the face beside me.

It was brown and fat and old yet somehow it suggested the innocent goodwill we like to associate with the young. There was an air of wonder about the round eyes and the full, ripe lips, parted most of the time as if she needed to breathe through her mouth. I had a feeling that I was looking at one of life's predestined victims.

Her body was full and ripe, too, and swathed in a shapeless calico smock. She sat back on her heels and said: "I ain't seen you on Beekman Street before. What are you doing here?"

"I was looking for somebody."

"Who?"

"A woman called Moon Mother."

As I said it, I knew what her answer would be. There was something of the full moon in her round, firm, golden-brown face, and her ample body looked maternal.

"Who done told you about me?"

"A man who thought you might know something about the girl who was kidnapped, Katherine Endicott."

The wonder in her face changed to fear.

"Who done this to you?"

"Some boys or maybe young men. I didn't get a good look at them. It was dark and everything happened quickly. They could have been sent by several people who don't like me."

"But they didn't kill you." She thought this over. "They could if they had wanted to. Why didn't they?"

"Perhaps they just wanted to . . . well, discourage me."

Fear surged into her eyes blotting out everything else. "I think they wanted to keep you from talking to me."

"Why?"

"I think they were some of Al's boys. Young kids who hang around the street here. He uses them when he wants somebody watched or roughed up. It's big stuff to them. Makes them feel like men."

I tried to sort out all the implications of this. Why would Al's boys watch me or rough me up unless . . .

"Do you know where Kate Endicott is?" I demanded.

"Not now."

109

"Do you know who is hiding her?"

"Sort of."

The light beyond the door was whiter now, but no brighter. This was going to be a gray day in a gray street where the sun could not penetrate even on clear days.

"Can you walk now?"

"I can try."

"Then we better get you outa here before people come around."

"Upstairs?"

"No, next door. Lean on me."

I got to my feet by pushing against the wall. Once I was up, her shoulder was steady as a rock under my head. We managed to stagger together out into the street and up the stairs of the building next door to the top floor.

Once I had to pause and rest. "What happened to the watchman?"

"He got beat up like you. I found him first and sent him home. He doesn't want anybody to know about this. Might lose his job. They'd fire him if they knew he left that door open, so I told him I'd lock up and leave a note saying I got the key. When the super comes for it, I'll tell him the guy got took sick. You ready to go on up now?"

"Yes."

We plodded on.

"Why did he leave the door open?"

She gave me a smile for the first time. "You like to know things, don't you? He had to slip out and meet a guy at the corner. He was only gone a minute or so."

That sounded like hash or heroin. I wondered if he had got it, or if he had simply been lured outside by a telephone call from people who wanted a chance to get at me.

Moon Mother's place was a real Manhattan loft, a whole floor with a high ceiling intended to house a workshop or small

110

factory. The first impression it made on the eye was one of space and height, openness and emptiness.

There was a sink and an oil cooking stove, no bathtub. Who wants a bathtub in a factory? Later I found there was an old-fashioned water closet on the ground floor that served the whole building.

Above the sink there were two shelves of food in jars and cans, mostly baby food and dog food and one carton of dry milk.

Beyond the sink was a shallow cupboard, its shelves empty, its door open. In front of it six or seven big cartons were stuffed with clothes and kitchen pots and pans, not unpacked yet. Apparently they were just moving in.

In the middle of the room stood a kitchen table and two chairs. They looked as if they had been there for a long time. They had lost all trace of paint.

In one corner a huddle of blankets made a nest on the floor. "Sit down."

I lowered myself gingerly into one of the two chairs. So far as I could tell there were no bones broken, but you can't always be sure about that until you see X-rays.

She was moistening her damp cloth at the sink. She was taller than I had realized, more muscular than fat. She was built on the heroic scale, Amazonian, but like so many big people she was gentle, as if she were mortally afraid of abusing her strength.

She was using the damp cloth on my forehead again. "That was done with a sap," she said.

"Was it?" I answered. "All I know is that something hit me and I went out like a light."

"You can't dodge them all," she said.

I thought: You can if you're young and in training and I am neither one now.

"Think you could manage breakfast?"

111

"Thanks, I'd like coffee."

"And I got some fresh milk here because of the boy. It was when I went out to get the milk that I found you."

"The boy?"

At the heart of the cocoon of blankets a small body was beginning to stir. A head turned, eyes opened and stared at me, but no words came.

"Who's that?" I asked.

"Al calls him Zombie because he can't speak. He hasn't spoken since the accident, so everybody calls him Zombie now."

"What was his name before?"

"Eddie, but don't call him that. It upsets him."

"He's your son?"

"My grandson."

"Where are his parents?"

"His mother died."

"And his father?"

"Lord only knows where that one is now. I don't want to know. He was bad medicine."

She was mixing hot milk and baby oatmeal in a saucer. "You hungry, Zombie?"

He nodded and sat up. He was painfully skinny, but there was still toughness and vitality in him. I soon learned that his eyes could express everything the rest of us express in words: joy and fear, laughter and rage, love and hate.

He had a good appetite. He held out his saucer for more.

She opened another jar for him and looked at me. "Want bread with your coffee?"

"Just coffee, please. I'm not quite ready for bread yet."

It was instant coffee, but hot and fragrant. I sat and sipped it with the sharp relish that comes only from need, and watched the dull light grow a little beyond window panes so greasy with smog that you could hardly see the houses opposite or the sky above them.

112

"How long ago was the accident?"

"Two years."

"Car?"

"Na-a, nothing like that. You know those blue movies? Not just sex, but rough stuff? They use children now and then. You can make real money that way, but sometimes there are accidents. Some guy gets all excited and hits a little too hard or . . . well, you can figure it out for yourself."

"And something like that happened to Zombie?"

"Yeah. He was too young, I guess. He was real upset for a while. He's okay now. You can see that. He's quite happy playing with his doll. He just doesn't talk. And he's afraid of Al. I didn't know what I was getting into when I took up with Al. Now I just don't know how to get shut of him. He doesn't like to let his people go."

"You haven't been here long?" I said, my eyes on the unpacked cartons.

"Not real long."

"Ever been in Connecticut?"

"We sticks around here mostly."

"Do you know Kate Endicott's mother is offering a reward of ten thousand dollars?"

Moon Mother gave me a long straight look. "Nobody's going to claim it."

I was impressed. Ten thousand would be a large sum to anyone in this neighborhood.

"You mean they'll be afraid to?"

She nodded.

I said what Satan must have said to Eve in Eden.

"No one would ever know."

She was less gullible than Eve. "They'd know. You can't hide money."

"Who is 'they'?"

Her eyelids dropped.

"Al Jebble and Foxy are the only ones I know. I've just heard

113

about the Old Man of the Mountain." She didn't look at me as she talked. She kept her eyes on the sink and her voice was lower than usual. "I wasn't in at the beginning. I didn't know anything about it until they brought her here and she's not here now. You can see that for yourself."

"She?"

"This girl you're talking about, Kate Endicott. Foxy brought her here and Foxy took her away."

"What is Foxy's full name?"

"Ellen Fox. Al calls her Fox Maiden. He's the one gave us all these funny names, like we was folks in a movie or something."

"I'm surprised he didn't call you Earth Mother."

"Oh, he explained all that. The real, old, first goddess of all was the moon. It had something to do with women being fertile once a month. Then folks found babies had fathers and they made a he-god of the sun, and the rain was his seed. They couldn't have two gods in the sky, so they said woman was earth, just made to hold male seed and keep it safe while it was growing. Now we know women have seed, too, we oughta go back to the old moon mother."

I could see that she took real pleasure in her name, Moon Mother, and I began to understand why this "Al" had given them these fancy names. No one knew better than I that you cannot change your name without changing your personality. As Moon Mother and Fox Maiden they could do things they would never be able to do as Mary Doakes or Jane Doe.

"Does Al himself have any other names?" I asked her.

"He likes to call himself Hassan-ben-Sabah."

"And his real name?"

"Al Jebble."

"Have you any idea where Fox Maiden is now?"

"I told you I'm not talking."

"If you don't the girl Kate may die. There isn't much time left."

"And your interest in her is just personal?"

"Very personal."

I saw compassion in her eyes. I held my breath.

When she finally spoke it came in a little rush as if she wanted to get it all out before she had time to change her mind.

"I don't know where she is. I know where she could be. She was there yesterday, but they move her around. I ain't going to write it down. You got to remember it. Uptown, East 14th Street, Number 423A. She—"

Her hearing was more acute than mine. It was several seconds after she stopped speaking that I heard the steps on the stairs.

Her voice was scarcely audible. "It's him now."

"Who?"

"Al."

12

There was no attempt to conceal the footfalls coming up the stairs. They marched, loud and resolute, from step to step as if they were deliberately calling attention to an important visitation in advance.

Moon Mother's glance flashed around the room and came to rest on the cupboard. She pointed and I moved faster than I would have thought I could a moment ago.

Now she was looking at the boy, one finger at her lips. He nodded and put a finger on his own lips, then dropped his eyes and went on dressing his doll. He might not be able to communicate with others but there was little he and Moon Mother could not say to each other.

I had stepped into the shallow closet. There was just room enough for me if I stood upright, my back pressed against the shelves so they dug into my spine, but damp and neglect had warped the unseasoned wood in the ill-made door beyond repair. I could not get it to shut entirely and I had no idea how much of me was visible through the crack between door and frame. I had a narrow, wedge-shaped view of the room that included the door into the hall.

The door burst open so violently that it hit the wall and bounced back and forth on its hinges for a few moments. In the doorway stood a commandingly tall man, deep-chested and hawk-faced, with a skin dark enough to emphasize the brilliant contrast of white teeth and eyeballs. Tangled hair hung to his shoulders and a ragged beard flowed over his breast. His eyes were brightly black and piercing as the eyes of Rasputin in old photographs.

He radiated an exuberant vitality that owed nothing to drink or drugs. I doubted if such a man would feel the need of chemical stimulants.

I remembered then that the leaders of the old Hashashin did not take hashish themselves. It was used to reward and dupe their corps of professional killers and there was a bold simplicity about this deception which had always fascinated me. It was an extreme form of pie in the sky.

After his first killing, the killer was doped and taken to a flowery Persian garden where he woke to every luxury and lascivious delight—music, wine, women, boys and more hashish. He was told that he was in Paradise and, because of the drug, he believed it.

In a few days he was returned to his own bare, narrow cell in a drugged sleep, but when he woke he still believed that he had been in Paradise. From then on he would commit any atrocity if promised another glimpse of Heaven and he would face any death for he believed that he would then return to his garden of delights forever. He had become the perfect instrument of death.

The line between deception and self-deception is so narrow I wondered just what the leader of the New Hashashin believed. Was he like the leader of the old Hashashin, a cynic using fools for his own ends? Or had he become the victim of his own propaganda? Did he now himself believe everything he had taught others? And who was the real leader? This Al, whom Moon Mother seemed to fear so much, or the Old Man of the Mountain whom she had never even seen?

"Anybody else been here?"

I knew that voice at once. It was the deep rich voice, vibrating like the hum note of a bass bell, which Adam, Isolda and I had first heard when we listened to the tapes.

It was then I realized what I should have realized long ago. If you pronounce "al Jebal" with an American stress on the first syllable and all syllables run together, it becomes "Al Jebble." It's the same difference you hear in the word "daiquiri" as pronounced by Mexicans and Americans.

"Na-a." Moon Mother's voice was bored, almost lazy. "just me and Zombie."

I, who had seen her agitation only a few moments before the door was flung open, marvelled at her self-command but only for a moment. Then I realized that she led a life where the art of dissimulation must be the first essential of survival.

"Sure?" His voice was growing abrasive.

"I'm sure and you know I wouldn't lie to you, Al."

"See you remember that." This was said casually, without passion, as if it were a ritual admonition.

I heard a rush of water, a clink of crockery and aluminum. She must be washing the breakfast dishes.

"That fellow I told you about, Joel, has been seen around here. If you see him, or hear anything about him, I want to know."

"What's he after?" Her voice was preoccupied. No trace of interest or even curiosity.

"Trying to find the girl, I suppose, but he'll never find her now."

"You mean she's . . . ?"

"Na-a, she's not dead, but she's where he'll never find her, and nobody else cares much where she is, except the cops."

"How come?"

"Her joining up with us cooked her goose. Now everybody thinks she killed her own father."

118

"But she didn't?"

I began to wonder if Moon Mother was asking these questions for her benefit or mine. I think now it was a little of both. She wanted to know what was happening and she also wanted to help me.

"Na-a."

"Who did kill him?"

"What would you say if I told you that I don't know?"

She laughed richly and comfortably. "I'd say you were lying. You don't have to be all that cagey with me, Al."

"I'm not being cagey. It's the truth. Even I don't know everything that's going on."

"Does anybody?"

"Only the big fellow."

"Who is this big fellow?"

"The Old Man of the Mountain. I told you about him." Now Al's voice changed. It took on the rhythmic chant I had heard before on the tapes. "He knows everything. He can do everything. He's God."

"Where do I find this God?"

"You'll never find him, woman. Not a chance. Think he'd bother with trash like you?"

"My God bothers with everybody."

"So you got a God of your own now? Our Hashashin God ain't good enough for you? You're getting too big for your boots. I gotta teach you a lesson."

I heard the blow. I opened the door of the closet. Before I could move, the little boy hurled himself at the man.

Al laughed, fending off the child with one hand. "Don't you get above yourself, Zombie!"

He raised his right hand and Moon Mother spoke in a new voice:

"Let the boy be."

Like all leaders, Al knew just how far he could go. All domi-

119

nation is a form of deception and the cardinal rule is: Never issue an order unless you are sure it will be obeyed.

Moon Mother had reached a point where she would stop at nothing to protect Zombie and Al knew it.

"Okay, okay," he conceded in an indifferent tone that minimized the importance of the incident and reduced the emotional temperature.

Moon Mother looked in my direction and saw I had opened the door. She shook her head. I pulled the door as nearly shut as I could.

Al was looking down at Zombie. "No hard feelings, eh, boy?"

The child dropped his eyelids and went back to his doll.

"I'd better be pushing off," said Al. He was working hard to reestablish good will.

Zombie wanted no part of it, but Moon Mother made an effort to meet him halfway.

"Like some coffee?"

"I got things to do."

"Coming back soon?"

"You'll see me when you see me."

Then he was gone.

I had been standing so long in such a narrow space I was as cramped and stiff as an old man when I came out.

Moon Mother eased me into one of the kitchen chairs.

"You'd better go soon as you catch your breath. He'll be back in half an hour or less."

"Do you think he saw—?"

"No, he didn't see you. He'd have taken you apart if he had. No, it's me he's getting suspicious of. He knows I don't like this kidnapping bit. Sometimes I don't know how I got in so deep. It all happened so sudden."

"Why don't you ditch him?"

"Where would I go? To the cops? They'd try to make me

120

turn him in. I couldn't do that. I hate him now, but I didn't always."

"Why not just get out and go as far as you can?"

"Using what for money?"

"Would a check for bus tickets to California be any help?"

"I got no way to cash checks. Now, if you could make it a money order . . ."

"I can do better than that. I'll send you cash. Get the boy to a doctor."

"I'll probably never pay you back."

"I know all about that. I've been broke, too."

I crossed to the window and rubbed one of the panes clean with my hand. I could see no sign of Al in the street below.

Moon Mother raised the window and leaned out to look.

"Okay. Better beat it while you can and, remember, he's tricky."

I left the subway at 14th Street and stopped at a cafeteria for a late breakfast.

I was just finishing my second cup of coffee when I looked up and saw Al Jebble at the other end of the room.

He was not looking over at me. He was apparently absorbed in the morning paper, but I do not believe in coincidence.

How had he managed it? Hindsight is always humiliating but I saw now that he could have managed it very easily. All he had to do was to wait on a lower floor in that loft building, watching from a window until he saw me leave by the front entrance and then simply fall in behind me. I had been so eager to get on with the job of finding Kate that I had not been wary enough.

Now I would have to lose him before I did anything else and that would use up precious time. I started walking.

We were passing the Empire State Building in file with at least a dozen other people between us when two men came up on either side of me and fell into step with me.

121

Not thugs. Respectable types in hats and dark overcoats.

"We're from the Agency," said one. "Our orders are to pick you up for questioning."

"How do I know you're from the Agency?"

He produced a card. I had no doubt of its authenticity. I knew what to look for.

"They have to talk to you," said the one on the other side.

"Whatever it is, it can wait," I answered. "You see that tall man in the khaki jacket and slacks without a hat? The man with the long black beard?"

"Yes, but—"

"He's involved in the Endicott kidnapping. You ought to pick him up for questioning."

They exchanged smiles past my face. The one on my left said quite amiably: "You really believe that?"

"It's true. He admits it."

"Oh, he'd say anything, that guy. He's quite a character, a pathological liar. You can't believe anything he says."

"You know him?"

"Al Jebble? Sure. You can forget about him. He's one of our paid informers. He's been with us, on and off, for years. It was Al who telephoned us a little while ago and told us where we could pick you up."

I looked towards Sixth Avenue. Al was already out of sight. Even if I could escape from these two men now, I would have no idea where to look for Al.

13

A lot of things were clear now. Al Jebble was what Stebbins would call a double agent, an opportunist, who ran with the hare and hunted with the hounds, a part of the Hashashin, but, simultaneously, a part of the Agency. The boys who had attacked me were simply part of a gang who worked for him.

They had probably been following me ever since I had appeared in Lamborn Street. After all, I had gone there to make contact with the kidnappers as soon as I found the Lamborn Street News Agency label sticking to the newspaper wrapper of the tape hurled through the window.

Why hadn't Agency men who worked for Al Jebble recognized his voice on the tapes?

There could be only one answer: the tapes had never been played to them and they had not been listening when the tapes were broadcast. Theoretically the Agency was restricted to foreign intelligence. There was no reason for Agency men to listen to broadcasts about domestic crime in general and Digby himself was far too high in the hierarchy to have had personal contact with Al Jebble.

If only he had, he could have arrested Al days ago, but, to Digby, Al was just one of many Agency stooges and stool pigeons, not Hassan ben Sabah, Sheikh al Jebal, second only to the Old Man of the Mountain himself in the leadership of the New Hashashin.

As for Al himself, he was not interested in me because I had once had an Agency connection. He was interested in me solely because I was a threat to the New Hashashin.

There was no casual conversation on a sunlit terrace for me at the Agency this time. The office where they took me now was bathed in a dull light from a low sky pregnant with rain.

It was the kind of office reserved for top brass in all government agencies, a big corner room with windows on two sides, a carpet thicker and redder than most and furniture too well-made to attract attention to itself.

There were the ritual personal touches: tortoise-shell cigarette box, silver-framed photograph of wife and children, fresh cut flowers in a crystal bowl. It was high enough for traffic noise to be reduced to a well-bred murmur, like the sound of surf at a distance.

There were no fatted calves in view, but I was offered a cigarette. I felt a little priggish explaining once more that I had given up smoking.

The man behind the desk was one I had met only a few times and then briefly. The Deputy Assistant Director of the New York Regional Office did not fraternize with the rank and file.

The other man, standing by a window, I did not recognize until he turned around. It was Digby.

It wasn't a shock to me to see Digby so suddenly because I was already in a state of shock. I was trying to adjust to the idea that Al Jebble was an employee of the Agency as well as a crook and that he must have followed me from Connecticut to Potter's Alley so skillfully that I had not detected him. Was he doing it for the Agency or for himself?

The man who followed Ghislain and myself in the subway had had no beard but he could have been a hanger-on of either

Al or the Agency. The fact that Ghislain and I had detected him and evaded him so easily suggested lack of skill and experience on his part.

And the attack on me in Beekman Street?

Once Ghislain and I had shaken off pursuit there was only one thing Al could do—assume that I would find Moon Mother eventually and set some sort of guard over her. The local adolescent gang was a good choice for the purpose. They would blend in with the landscape.

His own visit to Moon Mother that morning must have been an attempt to check up on the situation. He must have suspected that I was in the room while he was there or he would not have lingered in the building on another floor and followed me when I left.

His turning me over to the Agency by telephone told me one thing about him: He had a sense of mischief. He was enjoying this. I have always believed that crime is psychologically as close to the mischievous as it is aesthetically close to the grotesque.

The worst part of all this was the thought that if Al had known I was in the room this morning listening to his talk with Moon Mother, he might take it out on her. She could insist that she had had no idea who I was, but would he believe her?

The Deputy Assistant Director—I never could remember his name—was speaking to me now and I had missed the first part of his harangue. I only got the climax.

". . . we've been keeping an eye on you and we don't like what you're doing."

I started to speak, but he held up a hand.

"Apparently you are trying to find this girl who has been kidnapped. By so doing you have drawn the attention of the very people you should avoid at all costs, The Family."

"Are you sure?"

"Why do you think you were beaten up last night?" said

Digby. "Can you think of anyone else who would do that? I'm just surprised they didn't kill you. That would have been more logical. After all, you did infiltrate their narcotic setup in Vietnam."

"They may have been interrupted by someone or something before they could kill him," said the Director. "Or they may want some information that he has."

"About narcotics?" said Digby.

"Or about the Agency. That's why I had him brought here this morning." The Director turned back to me. "You know a great deal about the workings of the Agency, things The Family would like to know, such as the methods you used to subvert their organization in Vietnam. The possibility of your telling them about our methods and naming the identity of other agents still undercover is alarming."

"Why do you think I would tell them things like that?"

"We have reason to believe that you would break under intensive questioning."

"After all, you did in Vietnam," added Digby.

He wanted everything to be absolutely clear.

I would have loved to hit him, but I have learned to control these boyish impulses.

So I simply said: "Prove it."

"You know we can't." The Director leaned back in his comfortable armchair. "And you know we will always believe it. What we would really like is to have you disappear again. You could try Europe this time. Or South America. We'll even finance you again. It's worth that much to us to protect what you know or guess about our clandestine operations."

"So that's the real reason you wanted me to take a new name and identity the first time," I said. "Not to protect me, but to protect your secrets. I wonder if The Family is really as interested in me as you would like me to think, or have you exaggerated their vendetta against me to hold me in line?"

Before he could affirm or deny this, Digby broke into the conversation. "I'm here for another reason, Joel. Your activities are confusing the Endicott case. We don't think The Family was involved in the kidnapping originally, but they are taking an interest in it now and we think that's because of you."

"How do you know they're taking an interest?"

"A man named Lorenzo Visconti has been making inquiries about the case."

Did they know Enzo was a reluctant Mafioso? I wanted to protect him from both the Agency and The Family, so I said quickly: "My using that Agency money for part of the Endicott ransom payment is the only thing that interests The Family in the kidnapping. You warned me they would be interested if I spent it too soon. They're not quite sure yet that I was the one who queered their heroin deals in Vietnam, but they're suspicious now."

"All the more reason for your going to Europe or South America. What do you say?"

"No."

They had not expected this answer. They were not pleased with it.

"Can you give me one good reason why you shouldn't?" demanded the Director.

I couldn't, of course. The word love was not in their vocabulary. The silver-framed photograph of the Director's wife and children was a stage prop to flesh out the role he played in public. It had nothing to do with the way Kate and I felt about each other.

"Is there nothing we can say that will change your mind?" asked Digby. "Nothing we can offer you?"

For a moment I was tempted. It would be so much easier for me. With their manpower and other resources, they might find Kate much faster than I could alone. But then I remembered that television interview with Digby when he had spoken

127

so comfortably of a possible death penalty for Kate.

I could not bring myself to trust the man. I didn't want him to be the first one to question her after she was found in a weakened condition.

I think this was the moment when I finally decided that if I found her before anyone else I would take her directly to Carew in Connecticut. I trusted him.

So, once again, I said: "No, there is nothing you can offer me."

They exchanged glances without smiling. The Director brought his gaze back to me. "In that case we are going to wash our hands of you," he said. "We will not help you or protect you in any way no matter what happens."

"That sounds like a threat."

"Nothing of the kind. We are just saying that we will not protect you from those who are in a position to threaten you. Those men who beat you up last night are probably agents of The Family and they will probably seek you out again."

"You seem very sure of that."

"We are. Aren't you?"

"No, I don't believe it was men from The Family who attacked me last night." I turned to Digby. "I've been followed by a man called Al Jebble, and I think he's involved in the kidnapping. I pointed him out to the men you sent to pick me up just now, and they said this man is one of your paid informants. They even said Jebble volunteered to lead me to them so they could pick me up. Is that true?"

"It's true that Jebble is one of our paid informers. If the men said he was the one who told them where to find you, he probably is."

"And you trust him?"

"We don't trust people, we use them," said Digby. "Why are you so suspicious of this Al Jebble?"

"His voice sounds like the voice of the man who spoke on the two kidnapping tapes."

"I suppose we could run a voice-print test on him," said Digby.

"You should." The Director turned back to me. "Anything else about him?"

"I overheard him speaking of a girl. He said it would be impossible to find her, where she was hidden now. I think he meant Katherine Endicott."

"Why?"

"He mentioned that she had not killed her father. No one else is suspected of having killed a father. He talked about someone else he called the Old Man of the Mountain. That's what the old Hashashin in Syria and Iran called their leader. He ought to be questioned about these things."

"If we can find him," returned the Director. "He's capable of disappearing for weeks at a time."

Until that moment my one driving idea had been to get to Kate before anyone else did. Again I made myself face the unpleasant reality: No matter what individual mistakes these men made, an organization like theirs had a better statistical chance of finding Kate quickly than I did. I could check out the 14th Street address myself, but what about the other information I had? Wasn't I endangering Kate by holding that back? Wasn't she in greater danger from Al Jebble's cruelty and irresponsibility than from Digby's zeal and self-importance?

Digby would have to proceed against Kate in court where we could fight him. Al Jebble could end her life at any moment in circumstances where we could do nothing about it.

"Do you know where Al is now?" asked Digby.

"No, don't you?"

"The only address we've got for him is that loft on Beekman Street."

"I don't know of any other," I said. "I suppose you realize that if you have to besiege Beekman Street, you can't go in there with blazing guns. Too many people around. You might hit Kate herself if she were a prisoner there."

"What do you think we are?" Digby was indignant. "We don't operate that way. If criminals are holed up in a stronghold and won't surrender, we don't shoot, we talk them out of it. The technique is amazingly effective. Look at those recent cases in England and Holland. Why should we shoot if we don't have to? Besieged men break easily because they're prisoners, too. They're living in a confined space, under constant pressure, without adequate food, water and sanitation."

"Sounds almost as bad as being the victim of a kidnapping," I said. "They break easily, too."

He saw he had walked into a trap. He couldn't agree with me without going back on his contention that Kate's conversion to Hashashin doctrine had been voluntary, so he said nothing.

The Director intervened again. "What you really want to know is whether or not we plan to use violence against the kidnappers if we find them while Miss Endicott is still a hostage?"

"Exactly."

"I think I can promise you that nothing is further from our minds." He looked at Digby. "Can't I?"

"Of course. My men have strict orders to protect hostages at all costs even if it means a risk of the criminals escaping."

The Director looked at me again. "I'm beginning to see why you won't leave the country," he said. "It's the girl, isn't it?"

I did not want to talk to either of them about Kate.

I rose. "Are you through with me now?"

Digby shook hands with me, I suppose because I had given him some information.

The Director walked to the door with me like a good host. "We're grateful for what you've told us, but you do understand that, even if we wanted to, we can't protect you now unless you leave the country?"

"I'll take my chances."

When I left the elevator on the ground floor, I was not wholly surprised to see the one friend I had left here, Colonel Stebbins. If he knew that I was going to be in the building, he would try to see me.

He fell into step beside me, but didn't speak until we were in the street.

"Was it bad?" he asked.

"Not too bad." I told him all about it.

"You did the right thing to tell them as much as you did," he said. "They do have a better chance of finding her quickly."

I wasn't so sure I had done the right thing, so I changed the subject.

"What do you know about Al Jebble?"

"He's like all double agents, a con man. I doubt if he himself knows which side he's on now."

"Is that what he's called, a double agent?"

"That's what I call any man who works with criminals and against them at the same time. He invents half the things he tells us and why not? Why should he worry about truth if he can come up with lies we'll pay for? But he has one rule: He never tells us anything we don't want to hear."

"Did you just happen to be in the lobby when I got out of the elevator?"

Steb grinned. "You don't believe in Santa Claus? How right you are! I've been loitering with intent for nearly half an hour. I have a message for you from Ghislain de Boisron. Somebody you know as Fox Maiden has left the 14th Street address and moved to the Hotel Moxon on West 23rd. The message comes by courtesy of somebody named Enzo."

I put the slip of paper he handed me in my pocket.

"Thanks, Steb. This will save me time."

"Fox Maiden," he pondered. "Where do they get these names? Sounds Japanese."

"I believe her real name is Ellen Fox, but the Hashashin all take exotic names when they join."

"Split personality?"

"Maybe, or maybe just the practical advantage to any criminal of concealing his real identity. People are always saying how inventive and original crooks' slang is, but it's not a pure flight of creative imagination. It's strictly functional, a code for concealing plans from eavesdroppers in general and police and informers in particular."

I had something to think about as I walked to the nearest subway station. I knew where the Hotel Moxon was on West 23rd Street. It was respectable rather than fashionable and, for that very reason, I would be conspicuous if I went there scruffy and unshaven as I was now.

So there was nothing else for it. I had to go back to Potter's Alley to shave and change my clothes.

On the way I stopped at a barber's for a professional shave. I didn't believe I could tackle my chin bristles with an ordinary razor after this lapse of time. I also invested in a flask of brandy. I had a feeling I was going to need it before the night was over.

As I went down into the subway, I passed a newsstand and a familiar face caught my eye, Joey's face. It was a blown-up, photograph on the first page of one of those uninhibited tabloids that are supposed to appeal largely to the male.

MY LOVE LIFE WITH KATIE ENDICOTT

THE BURNING TRIBUTE OF KATIE'S ONE AND ONLY LOVER

JOEY ALFIERI TELLS ALL

And then, so there would be no doubt at all about the author:

BY JOEY ALFIERI

Those scandal rags go to town on publicity whenever they get hold of really hot stuff. If Joey could find a book publisher as well, he might make more out of this than the kidnappers.

When I came out of the subway in the Village, a sickly sun

132

was fighting its way through clotted clouds low in the west. By the time I reached Potter's Alley, it was quite a healthy sun sending long rays of golden light slanting down into the squalid street.

Just as on my first appearance there, silence fell the moment I arrived and the people on the front steps became so busy with whatever they were doing that they didn't have to look at me.

The mellow light searched out every scabrous detail of the defeated house where I was living. Its blistered, flaking paint looked like a skin disease. Its broken windows were cruel wounds. Even its sagging roof was like an old back cringing under blows.

When I entered the narrow vestibule, I was greeted again by an ancient smell of rotting timber, plumbing that had clogged and overflowed too often, and sweaty, unwashed bodies that had drifted in and out of the place for generations.

I didn't bother to shut the front door. The only lock in the house that worked was the one I had put on the door of my apartment upstairs.

As I reached the foot of the staircase, a rosy afterglow on the opposite wall vanished abruptly, and I was left in a thickening twilight, the beginning of darkness.

In that fading light I first became aware of how vulnerable I was to attack living alone in a deserted house. Suddenly I found it hard to keep myself from thinking about all those empty rooms. It would be so easy for anyone to walk in and occupy any one of them at any time without my being aware of it.

I was halfway up the stairs when I heard a sudden blast of music from above. It changed immediately to a voice talking, first high, then low.

I was not surprised to see that the lock on my door was broken. The sounds were coming from my apartment. I had no television or radio with me.

133

The voice was still loud enough to cover the sound of my footsteps, so whoever was in the room could have no idea that I was on the other side of the door.

I snatched it open and took a step into the room, expecting to see a gang of sneak thieves, vandals or squatters.

Shock stopped me in my tracks.

"For God's sake, what are you doing here, Isolda?"

14

The new lock on my door was a good one and it was still intact, but the rotten wood around it had given way. This was the method I would have used to force an entrance myself if I had wished to do so.

She was not surprised to see me.

"I'm sorry about the door, Sam. I thought I could manipulate the lock, but, when I put pressure on it, the wood just gave way."

"It doesn't matter. With a door as flimsy as that, a lock is not much use anyway."

She had set her portable television on a high shelf, pushing aside cans of food and milk to make room for it.

Now she reached up to turn the volume to zero. The noise stopped as if she had cut it off with a knife.

"You've just turned off the sound," I said. "The picture is still showing."

"I want it that way," she answered. "I want to know when the news comes on the air. I can tell if the picture is showing."

"How did you find this place?"

"I got it out of Captain Carew. Oh, yes, he knows what you're up to. He's worried about you."

Once again I began to long for a cigarette.

"Suppose you sit down and tell me about it," I said. "The cot's more comfortable than the chair."

"But I can't see the television set from the cot. I'll take the chair, if you please."

"I'm going to make a cheese sandwich," I said. "Would you like something to eat?"

She shook her head.

I made my sandwich and sat on the edge of the cot to eat it where I could not see the television screen. I had no desire to watch actors "mopping and mowing" in an unnatural silence like phantoms.

She hesitated, then made up her mind to be frank.

"Digby's been keeping an eye on you in New York. He told Carew."

Now I knew Al Jebble was one of Digby's tipsters, I saw how that could be.

"Digby." I let my voice dwell on the name with distaste. "The man who hinted on television that he'd like to see Kate tried in some jurisdiction where the death penalty was still in force. Apparently you would, too."

"I never said that. Only Digby said it and I think he's sorry now."

"He would be the moment his great heart discovered that such things are bad for his television image."

"I can't blame you for being bitter, Sam. I know I said things about Kate that I should not have said. I'm sorry, too. That's one reason I came to see you. So I could tell you."

"And what is the other reason?"

She eyed me as if I were an unpredictable force, like a fire or a hurricane, that might wreck everything at any moment.

"Sam, won't you please give this up?"

"Give what up?"

"Your attempt to find Kate. This is a job for professionals. You're not a policeman. You may get hurt. Or you may make the kidnappers so desperate that Kate herself gets hurt."

"And that would distress you, wouldn't it?"

"I said I was sorry about all that. Adam's death was a great shock to me. I didn't know what I was doing or saying for several days."

"In shock *veritas,"* I retorted. "It's part of the technique of cross-examination. If you can shock a witness, he'll blurt out the truth."

Isolda sighed. "All right. I won't talk about Kate. At least I hope you'll believe that I care a little about what happens to you. Adam was always fond of you. He wouldn't want to see you destroy yourself this way."

"If Adam was the man I think he was, he would gladly see me destroy myself if it saved his daughter. Besides, I was destroyed long ago."

"What do you mean?"

"You said I was not a professional cop, but I am a little more professional than you think. When I was with the army in Vietnam, I worked with the Agency. I never was a newspaper man until I got to Greenwood."

"Then . . . you didn't tell us the truth about yourself in Greenwood?"

"I used a cover story the Agency gave me. Ask Carew. I'm sure he knows all about it by this time."

If he did, he hadn't told her. She was troubled as well as surprised now, and I thought I knew why. She had come here believing she was going to deal with an unsuccessful newspaper man softened by his professional failure and resigned to it. Dealing with a former Agency man who still had contact with the Agency was quite another matter.

"So that's how you were able to get that fifty thousand for Adam," she said.

"I'm not giving up, Isolda." I spoke quietly now. "I am going to find Kate."

"Do you really believe you will find her unchanged? The same Kate you knew in Greenwood?"

"No," I answered soberly. "We all change under stress."

"Then why . . . ?"

I looked at her, wondering if I could make her understand, wondering even more why I wanted to make her understand.

She was not quite as collected and controlled as I had thought at first. The hair, once so carefully disarranged, was now really disarranged, tangled and unbecoming. Her shoes needed polish, one of her nails was broken. There was a stain that looked like coffee near the cuff-link on the shirt cuff that showed below the sleeve of her suit jacket.

In Isolda all these were signs of disintegration, but the erosion showed even more in her face and voice. The lines had coarsened around her mouth. Her voice had lost the cool assurance which had so impressed Carew and Digby during that first interview with her.

"I suppose it's the way I think about love," I said.

That really startled her.

"You love Kate?"

"Didn't you know? I thought everyone had guessed. Adam did."

"No, I didn't know. Oh, Sam, I am sorry. This is awful for you."

"And awful for Kate," I reminded her. "How do you suppose she felt when she heard what you said about her on television?"

"But would she hear that?"

"Of course. The kidnappers would see to that. You and Digby handed them weapons to use in breaking down her morale."

"Then you don't really believe she has changed?"

"What's change? When I was a child someone read me an old folk tale about a girl who was bewitched by a sorcerer and forced to assume one hideous shape after another. The sorcerer

138

told her lover he could break the spell if he could hold her through all the changes no matter how terrifying or disgusting they were.

"So he held her in his arms while she turned into a tiger, a snake, a rat, a dragon and many other creatures each more grotesque than the last, but always he held on and when he had held long enough the spell was broken and he had his love safe in his arms again, unchanged."

To me this had always seemed a perfect allegory of the love that displaces the ego and sees below the surface of life, but one look at Isolda told me I had wasted my breath. She was so much a daughter of her time, and this very old myth had come down to us from a culture that existed before time and self were invented. It was so archaic that I had heard it among the Montagnards of Vietnam, only there the pair were a mother and a child, not lovers.

"You're telling me that you won't give up your search for Kate?" said Isolda.

"That's it."

"No matter what I say?"

"No matter what you say. Why are you so anxious for me to give it up? I cannot believe that it's out of concern for me. Adam and I were friends, but he is dead and I don't believe you ever really liked me."

She had just lighted a cigarette. Now she dropped it on the floor and stepped on it to put it out for there were no ashtrays. Her face had changed now. She was looking as if she had decided to unleash a fury she had been holding back ever since I entered the room.

"You fool! You sentimental fool! How that little half-caste took you in! They're all whores, those Asiatic women, and—"

I tried to stop her. "Kate is Adam's daughter and—"

"And she'll inherit everything he had now he's dead. Have you thought about that? Maybe she got tired of living the way

139

she had to live with Adam in Greenwood. Maybe she realized Adam could have lived for another twenty years. Maybe she wanted fun and games now so she contrived her own kidnapping to get the money and shot and killed him because he had discovered that she was her own kidnapper. What do you think of that?"

"I think you are jealous of Adam's love for Kate. We have Biblical authority for the fact that jealousy is cruel as the grave."

Isolda was beside herself now. Her mouth was working, but no words came. With a shaking hand, she reached for another cigarette. She was looking at the television screen when she struck a match. She never did light that cigarette. Her hand froze in midair and the flame burned down the match until it scorched her fingers and she had to blow it out, her gaze still on the screen.

So I left the cot and stood where I could see the screen myself.

There were some police in uniform. There were more men in plain clothes. They were hurrying down a city street.

I turned up the volume.

". . . holed up in an old loft building on Beekman Street," said a voice offscreen. "It is now believed that Katie Endicott's kidnappers are inside and that Katie herself may be there . . ."

I lost the rest as Digby's face came on screen.

"We believe we have the whole gang surrounded," he said.

"Including Katie Endicott?" That offscreen voice must be from a network interviewer.

"Including Katie Endicott." The satisfaction in Digby's voice was apparent. "We've had them under siege for nearly two hours."

"What happens now?"

"That depends on them. We'd like to talk them into surrendering, of course, but at the moment they don't seem responsive to verbal persuasion."

140

It was a night of cloudy darkness. Street lamps made little impression on the shadows and there were none of the strong lights television men usually employ for outdoor scenes after dark. The police searchlights picked out a face or a figure here and there, but mostly the picture on screen was shifting, flickering, ill-defined and distorted as a bad dream. There were some lighted windows and headlights from cars but they only seemed to add to the shadowy confusion.

At last a searchlight was turned on a building and I saw what I had been dreading to see: the loft building where I had talked to Moon Mother and Zombie only a few hours ago.

I thought of Precious Jade and prayed she was not watching this. I thought of Digby's elaborate assurance that guns would not be used to recapture Kate. Isolda was right. I was a fool. I should have known Digby would lie.

I glanced at her. She did not look happy now. After all she was not used to physical violence. Words, yes, but not blows or bullets. She had one hand at her mouth as if she were sealing a scream inside.

Digby's voice droned on. I hardly listened. I had never felt more helpless in my life. It would take me thirty or forty minutes to get to Beekman Street and what could I do when I got there?

But I had to try.

I was on my feet.

"Where are you going?" cried Isolda.

"Out."

I was halfway to the door when the sound of a shot tore through the room.

I was too late. Nothing I could do now. I didn't look at the screen. The sounds were enough.

There were more shots. A strange voice was telling us that there was no one in the building but the criminals and they had fired first so the police had no choice but to return the fire in self-defense.

141

"Oh . . ." moaned Isolda. "They've set the place on fire."

"A stray shot probably hit the oil stove," I said.

At last I looked. Smoke shot with flame billowed across the screen. There must have been a high wind. I heard the clangor of fire engines on their way.

"They probably didn't mean to set fire to the building," I said.

"You're defending them?"

"No, merely trying to be just. Their fault was in returning that first wild shot. They should have given persuasion more chance, but somebody panicked. Probably Digby."

"Why?"

"This case meant a lot to his career. He would have lost face unless something was done quickly. It's a case that is charged with emotion for most people because so many parents and children are having troubled relations with one another today."

Even to my own ears my voice sounded inhumanly detached.

I had reached that further side of anguish where we feel nothing at all. Either Kate had burned to death and it was all over or she was somewhere else and still alive.

This outburst of violence would raise the emotional temperature of everyone involved so it was more urgent than ever that I should find her before anyone else did.

I was trying to make myself believe that Moon Mother and Zombie had not been trapped in that burning building, but I knew they were more likely to have been there than Kate. I was sure they would not have fired the shot that started everything, but suppose Al had been there with them?

I moved towards the door.

"You're leaving me alone here?" cried Isolda.

"You were alone here when I arrived."

"It was different then." She looked towards the dark windows, but I don't believe it was the night that troubled her. She was thinking about what she had seen on screen.

"If you want to leave with me, you'll have to be quick," I said. "I'm in a hurry."

She didn't ask where I was going or what I was going to do. We were no longer on terms like that. I forgot completely that I had come back here to shave and change. It was no longer important.

We walked in silence until we came to lower Broadway, where there were taxis. I hailed one for her.

She leaned forward while the door was still open. "Sam, please try to forgive me."

"I can't." I shut the door and took the subway to 23rd Street.

Fox Maiden was my last hope.

15

I knew the neighborhood around Madison Square well, for when my parents came back from Japan in their old age they had lived at the little Madison Square Hotel. Today those high-ceilinged rooms, overlooking leafy tree-tops in summer, are only a ghostly memory. In their place stand office buildings as oblong and inhuman as filing cabinets.

Twenty-third Street, like Fourteenth, is a cross-town artery and west of Fifth Avenue it becomes a street of small neighborhood shops, snack bars and taverns, cafeterias and pizza parlors. As I came up out of the subway I was greeted by a glare of neon and a blare of canned music from a radio and television shop at the corner.

No one was listening to the sounds or looking at the colored lights. People in the street were sober figures going about their business in a preoccupied state, hardly aware of anything around them.

As I got nearer to the Hudson River the small shops and dingy bars began to give way to modern apartment buildings and old brownstone houses converted into flats with here and there a small hotel. People who lived here would not say they lived on West 23rd Street. They would say they lived in Chelsea.

It was on the edge of this neighborhood that I found the Hotel Moxon. It was a far cry from that other hideout of the Hashashin, the loft on Beekman Street. It looked like dozens of other small hotels between Washington Square and 59th Street. Outside the ground-floor facade had been modernized cheaply with floodlights, chromium, a sheet of plate glass, and a dado of plastic trying to look like marble.

Inside there was a lobby, circa 1900, with a high ceiling, sure to double fuel bills, and panelled walls, the wood so dark and so intricately carved that it would take hours to dust.

Perhaps that was why the floodlights were reserved for outside. Here, in the lobby, a few twenty-five-watt bulbs turned night into twilight and made it impossible to read. It occurred to me that in this uncertain light no one was going to stare at my shabby clothes. I would have been more conspicuous if I had not been able to shave. Beards are fashionable at the moment, but I know of no time or place where a bristly chin is not regarded with suspicion.

I crossed a spongy, fitted carpet to the reception desk and asked for "Miss Fox."

The clerk lifted his eyes from a ledger and glanced at a row of letter-boxes behind him to see if her key was there.

"She's in," he said. "You can announce yourself on the house phone, 1041."

His eyes went back to the ledger.

I walked past the shelf of house extension telephones to the elevators. They were unmanned and I had one all to myself. I pushed the button marked "10." The car creaked upward with the arthritic lethargy and shakiness of a really old elevator.

The tenth-floor corridor needed painting and cleaning. This place was a sinking ship. The bulldozer and demolition ball would soon move in to mash one more solid, decent, old building and replace it with something so shoddy that there would be a large yearly tax deduction for rapid depreciation.

I walked down the corridor on a strip of sisal matting and knocked on a door marked "1041."

A voice sang out: "I told you not to bring the drinks until eight o'clock and—"

The door swung open. The voice died. When she spoke again, she was an octave lower.

"Who are you? What do you want?"

Was this the voice that spoke the last line on the first tape made by the kidnappers? Hard to tell for this time it was not hoarse and it was not shaking with triumphant malice. It was just peevish.

Before she could move to shut the door I stepped across the threshold. I was close enough to see her pupils dilate. New Yorkers scare easily these days and the last thing I wanted was a frightened girl on my hands, but I wasn't going to let her lock me out.

I gave my voice a tone of bored indifference that should have reassured her and said: "Moon Mother gave me your address."

She was not reassured. She took a step backward and whispered: "How could she?"

"What do you mean?"

"Don't you know Moon Mother is dead?"

There could be only one explanation. "You mean she was killed in the shoot-out?"

"Or burned in the fire that followed it. She and Zombie both. There wasn't much left of them. The bodies were so charred they could tell age and sex only from the bones."

There was a question I had to ask, but my lips were suddenly so stiff it was hard to shape the words.

"Anyone else dead?"

"No."

"Are you sure?"

"Of course. It was on the news and then Al phoned me. He has an in with the Agency so he can get information like that and—" She cut herself short. "How do you know Moon Mother? Who are you?"

I looked about the room. It was cheaply modern but it was cheerful and clean and spacious. There were windows on the street. The bathroom and kitchen were small but adequate.

"You live a lot better than Moon Mother," I said.

"Don't you know that each of us has to pay his own way out of earnings? I'm white and single. Moon Mother is black and she has Zombie. So I earn more and I have more to spend on myself."

"You don't share and share alike? I thought one purpose of the New Hashashin was to redress inequalities."

She was on the defensive now and she had to tell me all about it.

"That's what I told Al, but he said I was being impractical. Once we have changed society itself, then Moon Mother and everyone else will have a decent place to live, but while we're in this transition stage, fighting for the change, the leaders must have conveniences like telephones and so forth."

I could hear Al saying this. I was beginning to understand his role in the Task Force of the New Hashashin. He was the realist you find in every political organization, right or left, the man with nothing on his mind but personal ambition. He had gathered around him a group of romantics whom he could control by a few trigger words: brotherhood, social justice, economic democracy, all concepts that meant everything to his followers and nothing to him. He was like the atheist priest who does not believe a word of his own sermons, and the augurs of ancient Rome who used to wink at each other when they met in the streets.

I had suspected this the moment I heard he was a paid informer for the Agency. Now I had met Fox Maiden, I was sure of it.

She was not at all like the symbolic Fox Maiden in the

147

Japanese Record of Ancient Matters: "A great fox with nine tails and hair like gold wire, the Precious Perfection who brought ruin to the Great Princes of Ancient Cathay."

She was little and thin and stringy. The straight, drab hair that hung below her waist was thin, too, and rather greasy. Her skin was so white that, even in a city where sun rays had to be filtered through smog most of the time, she had a spatter of freckles across her high-bridged nose. Her face was pinched and narrow, her lips thin, her eyelids a little red along the edges from some chronic conjunctivitis.

A loose peasant blouse and flowing cotton slacks hung on her bony frame like old garments on a broomstick scarecrow. Her feet were bare and so inevitably dirty in a city as filthy as New York.

But there was more to her than all this. Something in the way she moved and spoke and used her eyes betrayed the fanatic. She was so very sure of her own righteousness and so equally sure of the unrighteousness of other people.

Fifty years ago she would have been working to make Prohibition a Federal law. Two hundred years ago she would have been testifying against a witch in Salem. The causes change, but the temperament is unchanging, and it has destroyed many worthy movements it has advocated by its rigidity in both theory and practice.

"Unfortunately Moon Mother and Zombie didn't live beyond the transition period," I said.

"Was that our fault? That was the fault of the pig cops. Al says Moon Mother and Zombie had to be sacrificed. What do two people matter compared with the millions who will be better off once we've changed society, as we shall in a few more years?"

I looked at her sharply and saw that she really believed that the Hashashin could change society "in a few more years." She was far more removed from reality than I had realized and the possibility that Kate might be in her custody was unnerving.

She had lost her first fear of me now. She was lolling back on a studio couch, a feather of smoke rising from the burning cigarette between her fingers.

"You don't like violence, do you? Can't you see that political violence is necessary when all else fails?"

"No. I am tired of romantics who attack violence abroad and welcome or, at least, tolerate it at home. I believe that the resort to violence is the reason so few revolutions obtain their objectives. Do you really believe that Voltaire and Rousseau wanted the Terror? Or that Marx wanted a Stalinist state? Do you think Washington and Jefferson would be happy with some of the things we've done lately?"

"But they couldn't foresee—"

"Why not? Life is a chess game, and those who shape the future should be able to see at least a few moves ahead."

She crushed her half-smoked cigarette in an ashtray and lit another.

"You haven't answered my question. Why are you here?"

"Can't you guess?"

Her eyes narrowed as she waited for me to go on.

"I am looking for Kate Endicott," I said. "Either you or Al must have her now. I think it's you."

She laughed a high, harsh, artificial laugh. "Where am I supposed to be hiding her? Search the place. Go ahead. There's only the one room here with a kitchen and bath."

It is folly to ignore a bold challenge like this for there's always a chance it may be a bluff. So I did search, opening cupboards and closets, looking into the kitchen and the bathroom while she watched me with malicious glee. I even opened windows to make sure there were no balconies or fire escapes outside.

"What do you do in case of fire?"

"There's a fire escape at the other end of the corridor on this floor. It leads down into a courtyard. Nothing there but garbage cans and a board fence with a door into an alley."

I knew I could not search the whole building without backing from the New York police or the Agency, but I had a nagging feeling that Kate was more likely to be in this building with Fox Maiden now than anywhere else. Al seemed to have no fixed abode. Moon Mother's place was burned down. The Old Man of the Mountain was as intangible as a mirage. Where else could Kate be except with Fox Maiden?

In spite of the chromium and plastic marble out front, this was an old building and old buildings in New York have many secrets and surprises.

So there seemed to be only two alternatives: Get the Agency to search the building or persuade Fox Maiden to tell me where Kate was.

Neither was attractive. Fox Maiden would not persuade easily. She was the type who would burn at the stake without revealing a thing, revelling in her moral superiority to her persecutors. The Agency would bring in Digby, who was committed to the idea that Kate was a voluntary member of the Hashashin just as criminal as the rest of them. He needed that now to distract attention from his role in the shoot-out.

So in the end I decided to try a third strategy: trickery.

First I tried to see if there was any heart left under the fanaticism.

"Did you watch the shoot-out?" I asked her.

She nodded.

"Can you imagine what watching that must have been like for Kate's mother, not knowing whether Kate was in the building or not?"

"I didn't know she had a mother."

"She has one living in Brooklyn."

For a moment that bothered her. Then she rallied.

"The social value of the maternal role was greatly exaggerated in Victorian times. Today we see the mother as the jealous castrater of sons and inhibiter of daughters. Children are better without mothers."

"You believe that?"

"Of course." She looked at me in amazement. "Are you questioning modern psychology?"

She spoke as if I had blasphemed and I saw that she was one of those who bring an essentially religious mind to scientific and social theory. She was not a fanatic after all. She was a fundamentalist.

Was she the woman who had burst through the screen door the night of the kidnapping that now seemed so long ago? I tried to visualize her in a long, limp dress with a stocking pulled down over head and face, but I couldn't. The face is so important that a mask makes identification almost impossible. She was thin enough to have been that woman, but not, I thought, tall enough.

"I think you and I had better get things straight," she was saying. "I'm a member of the Hashashin and all my sympathies are with them. After the shoot-out, the other side hasn't a leg to stand on."

"The police claim the Hashashin fired first."

"They would. Can you see Moon Mother firing on a policeman?"

"No, but I don't think she was alone with the boy there. I think Al was there. I think he fired the first shot and got out when he ran out of bullets."

"Why would he fire the first shot?"

"Perhaps he wanted to get rid of Moon Mother. She was unhappy about the kidnapping. He might see her as a weak link in his chain."

"I don't believe it. I believe Moon Mother and Zombie gave their lives gladly for a cause they believed in whether Al was there or not."

151

"You think Al's incapable of murder? Then who killed Adam Endicott?"

"Maybe your precious Kate killed her own father. Al didn't. None of us did. You're not really one of us, are you?"

"You thought I was?"

"You said Moon Mother gave you my address."

"She did."

"Then who are you?"

"I am a friend of Kate Endicott's."

"And you just can't accept her conversion to the Hashashin, can you?"

"No."

"Then who made the tapes?"

"Al and you."

"But Kate's voice was on them, too, identified by voice-prints."

"She followed the classic pattern of most hostages. First she was stunned with shock. Then deprivation, forced passivity and the constant fear of death at any moment made her as submissive and suggestible as if she had been hypnotized."

"You're saying we hypnotized her? We did not!"

"People hypnotize themselves in solitary confinement."

"How did you know we kept her in solitary confinement?"

"I didn't know. I guessed from the way she has been behaving."

Fox Maiden lit another cigarette and tossed back the long, greasy strands of hair from her shoulders.

"You're smart, aren't you? You've got a lot of stuff out of me, but you're not quite smart enough to understand Kate. She's through with people like you. She's just as much a member of the Hashashin as I am."

"There's one way to convince me. Take me to Kate now. Let me hear it from her own lips."

"I said you were smart, but you're not really. You can't be

152

fool enough to think I'd take you to Kate now."

"Why not?"

"And give you a chance to grab her and carry her off? Like hell!"

I rose.

"You going?"

"There's no point in my staying now."

"What are you going to do?"

I allowed myself to smile. "Wouldn't you like to know?"

I was halfway to the door when she called after me: "If you're going to call the police or the FBI or the Agency, you'll be sorry. They'll never get Kate alive, I'm warning you."

I opened the door and turned to take a last look at her. Considering the amount of trouble she had caused or helped to cause, she was a strangely ineffective figure, with petulant mouth and hard, ignorant eyes. It is not our masks of flesh that are either ugly or beautiful. It is the expression which molds them into significant form.

"Who is this Old Man of the Mountains whom Al talks about?" I asked her.

"I don't know. Al's the only one who's ever seen him."

I was halfway down the hall when I heard her door slam. I turned to look. The corridor behind me was empty.

The sisal matting muffled my footsteps as I walked to the other end of the corridor. I opened the door that led to the fire escape, closed it behind me, and hurried down the iron steps to the bottom. It was an old-fashioned device; the last flight of steps was actually a ladder hoisted above the paved court below. When you stood on it, your weight made it descend.

I jumped the last few feet to the ground and the ladder, relieved of my weight, rose again. I stood by the wall under the fire escape where I could not be seen by anyone coming down.

When I left so abruptly I had tried to give her the impression I was up to something. I wanted to give her the feeling that an attack was imminent and I thought I had succeeded. If you expect an attack your first thought is to check the safety of your most prized possession—children, money, jewels, papers, whatever it may be. Unless all my assumptions and calculations were wrong, Fox Maiden's most precious possession at this time was Kate.

She would check Kate's security, or move Kate elsewhere, as soon as I was gone. She would expect me or someone with me to watch the front entrance to see if she left the building. So if she had to leave the building to check on Kate, she would use the only back way.

I decided to give her five minutes, counting them second by second since I had no watch with me. They were the longest five minutes I have ever experienced and they were wasted, for Fox Maiden did not appear.

There was only one probable answer. She did not have to leave the building to check on Kate.

There was one other possibility that I did not want to think about. She might have taken Kate out of the building by the front way while I was being so clever watching the back way. If a prisoner is doped he or she can be moved through almost any crowd today as an invalid or a drunk.

I left the alley and went back to the front of the building. The clerk at the reception desk didn't even look up as I walked in. I glanced at Fox Maiden's mail box. A key was still there but that was not proof that she was still in the building. She might have two keys. It did make the possibilty that she was still in the building a little more probable.

Small as the probability was I had a sudden sense of excitement. The very thought that I might really be so near Kate at last after all that had happened quickened my whole being with joy and I felt as if I could do anything, however dangerous.

It is a curious heritage of our species, this trait that brings elation with danger. It must be a survival trait, useful to our

154

species in nature, but in civilization it can be suicide for the individual. Poor Oscar Wilde said of his homosexuality: "The danger was the most exciting part."

When I left the elevator, the tenth-floor corridor was empty again, but I could see a line of light along the threshold under Fox Maiden's door. There was a faint sound of music from inside, but no other sounds. Had she left the television or radio on so that anyone listening would think the room occupied when it was really empty?

Or was she lying on her studio couch at ease listening to the music?

Was she still expecting someone to come for drinks at eight o'clock?

At the opposite end of the corridor from the fire escape I noticed another door without a number, but there was no sign above it that said "Fire Exit." Was it just a broom closet? Or perhaps a stairway? This building was old enough to have had stairs before there were elevators.

As I was looking at the door, it began to open.

I stepped back of the elevator cage where I could see without being seen.

Fox Maiden came into my range of vision walking towards her own door. She was frowning, apparently worried. She let herself in with a key. So I had been right about some things. There were two keys and she had left a radio or television going so that any passerby would assume the room was occupied.

Her door closed. Music ceased. Then came a sound of running water, probably a shower.

I walked down the corridor to the door that had no number. There was no lock. It did not lead to a broom closet or a stairway. It led to another corridor, narrower than the first one, without any carpet, lit by one dirty unshaded bulb and cold as outdoors.

Quarters for domestic staff in the old days when they all

155

lived in? Rooms the hotel deserted and allowed to run down because there weren't enough hotel guests these days?

I had been right about one thing. There were secrets and surprises in old New York buildings.

I started walking down the corridor. There were no doors and no windows. It seemed like a passage between two buildings that had no function except to join them.

It turned a corner at a right angle and grew even narrower. Here the only light came from the one dim bulb I had left behind when I turned the corner, so it was almost impossible to see anything. I groped my way along until I came to the end of the corridor and another door so disused and derelict that I was surprised when the knob turned and I found I could push it open.

After the long walk down the devious passage, windowless as a tunnel, it was a little shock to come out into a room with windows so suddenly.

Such architectural absurdities are usually rooted in some legal absurdity: a cloudy title to land, a disputed right of way, a contested will or tax litigation. Of all I had ever seen, this fire trap was the worst. It could never have been let to normal tenants, but it could be let readily enough to people with something to hide. Later I found out that the hotel had let it as storage space. They had no idea anyone was living there.

The windows did not look out on 23rd Street. They looked out on one of the north-south avenues where stop-light changes are in phase with the speed limit so that anyone sticking to the speed limit can tear along without stopping at all.

Those avenues are wider than most streets. On the other side there were only office buildings where there would be no one at night and only busy people by day, people too busy to be curious about anything happening across the street.

The room seemed even colder than the corridor, perhaps because of the two windows. There was no light here except

156

a faint glow from street lights far below filtered through dirty window panes. There was one advertisement of moving lights across the way reflected on the ceiling in monotonously repetitive flashes, first red, then green.

As my eyes grew accustomed to the light I began to see more detail. There was an old-fashioned iron bedstead that had once been painted white. There was a bird's eye maple bureau, circa 1870. There was a wash stand of the same period with a pitcher, bowl, slop jar and chamber pot in china. There was a worn rug underfoot gritty as sand with an accumulation of city dust.

I took another step into the room and became conscious of a smell which I associated with active service. The smell of sweaty clothing, unwashed bodies, dung and urine.

There was a door on the other side of the room. Another room? A closet?

I opened it.

She was lying on the floor, her knees drawn up to her chest. Her ankles and wrists were bound. There was a gag in her mouth. Her beautiful black hair was bleached and dyed an unnatural and unbecoming shade of red. Her eyes were closed, but she opened them when she heard the door and I saw intelligence there as well as life.

I knelt on the floor and took her in my arms and kissed her.

PART THREE

Last Stand

Changeling . . . a child secretly exchanged for
another in fancy or supposed, in popular superstition,
to have been exchanged for another by fairies or elves . . .

Webster's New International Dictionary, Second Edition

16

The important thing was to get her out of there as quickly as possible. There was always the possibility that Fox Maiden might return and she might not return alone. She was expecting somebody for drinks at eight and it might be Al.

So I didn't even stop to give Kate coffee from the thermos flask or to wash her face and hands or to reassure her with words. I simply cut her bonds and took the gag from her mouth and thanked God that she was half Vietnamese and therefore small-boned and lightweight enough for me to carry her.

I wrapped her in my raincoat so that only the top of her head and the tips of her feet showed. I carried her as easily as I would have carried a child down the narrow secret corridor, through the door into the hall and through the door at the other end to the fire escape.

She didn't speak but I could feel that she was trembling.

I carried her down the fire escape as far as the ladder. I set her down on the last landing and used my own weight to depress the ladder until it touched the ground. Then I turned towards her holding out my arms.

"Jump. We haven't a moment to lose."

Without hesitation she launched herself into space and I caught her.

I carried her across the yard and down the alley. Now came the critical moment. I could not carry her in the street without attracting far too much attention. This avenue was neither residential nor theatrical. Its office buildings were closed and any taxis here at this hour would flash past us already loaded with passengers bound for uptown restaurants and night clubs.

Then I remembered that there were cross-town buses around the corner on 23rd Street. If they were still running at this hour they would not be crowded.

"Can you walk to the corner?"

She nodded.

I tucked her arm through mine. "Lean on me."

We only had to wait three or four minutes before a bus came along. Now I blessed the hippies and their negligent dress. Muffled in a man's raincoat much too big for her, barefoot, dirty and disheveled, she didn't attract any attention at all.

We found a seat for two that we could share. I put an arm around her and whispered: "Don't worry. Everything is all right now. We can get a taxi on Fifth."

She nodded, but still she didn't speak.

That was when I first became aware of the extent of her passivity. She had shown no surprise. She had asked no questions. She had accepted every suggestion I made and she had not spoken once. She was like a sleepwalker.

I remembered hearing that hypnotized subjects are sometimes so pliant and unresisting that they can be moved around as if they were mechanical dolls. Their minds become like the minds of very young children: "plaster to receive and marble to retain."

It was only after we left the bus at 23rd and Fifth and found a taxi that I began to have any feeling of safety. Even after I had told the driver: "Brooklyn—26 Jefferson Place" I found I could not relax completely. I kept watching his rear-view mirror.

Not that the mirror showed much. It had begun to rain and

162

everything behind us was blurred. All I could really see were golden headlights behind us in our own lane and crimson taillights ahead of us in the other lane. The wet had turned the asphalt into black glass so that it reflected the lights as if they were bright jewels.

In Jefferson Place I didn't wait for change. I just handed the taxi driver a handful of bills and helped Kate across the courtyard to the old carriage house. I wanted to carry her again but I didn't. The taxi man would notice and remember something like that and I didn't want to leave a string of traces along our trail if I could help it.

It was Ghislain who opened the door when I rang. He took one look and stepped back. He was always quick-witted. He knew she would have no idea who he was. He knew that once she identified him she might have little reason to like him. After all he was the man for whom her mother had left her father and herself.

We reached the top of the stairs. Precious Jade, sitting near the fire, put down a book and looked up.

She uttered one wordless cry and ran towards Kate.

The wet, dirty raincoat of mine that Kate was still wearing left dark streaks on the pale silk of Jade's dress, but she didn't notice. She was crying and kissing Kate.

Kate's state of suspended animation was protecting her now. Did she recognize Jade? I couldn't tell. It was years since they had seen each other. Kate was accepting Jade as passively as she had accepted me.

I handed my thermos flask to Ghislain. "Coffee. Give her some."

The big cap of the flask was also a cup. He unscrewed it, filled it with coffee and held it to Kate's lips. She sipped it obediently, but still she didn't smile or speak.

"Oh, she's filthy!" Jade was pulling off the raincoat. "Ghislain, please run a hot bath!"

He went down the hall. Jade followed with Kate. I heard

163

water running and a low murmur of voices—kind, loving, civilized voices, welcoming her back to the world she had so nearly lost.

A door closed, shutting off the sounds. Ghislain had come back into the living-room. He poured cognac for both of us without bothering to ask me if I wanted one.

His voice wavered over his next words.

"Did you tell her that her father is dead?"

"Not yet. I couldn't."

"Do you think they—the Hashashin—told her?"

"I don't know. She doesn't volunteer anything. She doesn't talk at all."

So I told him in rather jerky, rambling sentences just what had happened.

"You had luck," he said. "But only because you went out and looked for it. That's the only way anyone ever finds it. Have you any idea what this means to Jade?"

"I think I can guess."

"If Kate had died or disappeared forever, Jade could never have forgiven me for it was through me she lost her daughter."

I wanted to ask him more about it, but I didn't. Any sexual disaster leaves a deep wound and, unlike most psychiatrists, I believe such wounds should be allowed to heal in peace if possible. However, Ghislain must have read questions in my eyes for he went on: "You're wondering why Adam ever let Jade go?"

"I can't help wondering. You don't have to tell me."

"Adam was trying to prove something to himself when he married Jade. He was trying to prove that he had no racial prejudices, but he didn't really know himself. Who does? He had enough prejudice to make the marriage quite impossible and it was a tragedy for all three of them—Adam, Jade and Kate. Jade left Kate with Adam only because she thought it was best for Kate. I thought then she was wrong. I still do. But I

164

am damn glad she has got Kate back . . . if she has."

My glass was halfway to my lips. I put it down. "Just what do you mean by that?"

"I have not seen Kate since she was a small child," said Ghislain slowly and carefully. "You have. Are you sure that this young girl is really Kate and not a changeling?"

"Of course I am sure."

But even as I said it I knew I was not.

I had scarcely looked at her when I found her or when I bundled her into my raincoat and hurried her out of the place where she had been imprisoned. I couldn't really see her in the dim light of the bus and the taxi. I hadn't even tried to talk to her with the taxi driver listening. She had not volunteered a word so I had not heard her voice at all. Exhaustion, fear and possibly drugs were enough to explain her lethargy, but couldn't that lethargy be explained just as readily as a trick to conceal the substitution of another girl for Kate? The Kate I knew had always been so alert, so responsive . . .

"Jade has no doubts," I protested.

"Jade doesn't want to have doubts," he answered. "She's been in hell for days reproaching herself for ever having left Kate with Adam. Now you walk in with a girl who is exhausted, in a state of shock, perhaps even drugged. Of course Jade accepts her as Kate now, but what will happen in the next few days when this girl is clean and fed and rested, safe and secure and sure of herself? Will she seem like Kate then?"

"What would be the purpose of such an imposture?" I demanded. "No girl could arrange such a thing alone. Who would help her and why?"

"Suppose the real Kate died of shock or injury. That would make the kidnappers guilty of murder and they would lose all hope of collecting any more ransom money. But if they could produce a plausible surrogate for Kate and let us have a glimpse of her now and then, they might go on collecting money indefinitely and avert the charge of murder.

"Her alleged conversion to the Hashashin ideology would explain why she stayed with them instead of coming home to us."

"And then I come along and ruin everything by rescuing her?"

"That's one possibility. Another is that you were meant to rescue her. The Hashashin might see even greater advantage in planting a changeling devoted to their interests in the household of Kate's mother. At the least they could probably count on regular financial contributions from her."

"If she is an impostor, why was she gagged and bound and filthy when I found her?"

"To convince you and us that she was a prisoner and not a member of the Hashashin."

"Then Fox Maiden was baiting a trap for me all along?"

"It's possible."

"But it's so bizarre."

"These people are bizarre. That's their style. And Jade's offering a reward told them there was someone else willing to pay money for Kate's safety even after Adam was dead. Does the girl seem like Kate to you?"

How could I answer? It was hard to be objective when I so wanted her to be Kate, but I tried.

"The loss of weight and the dyed hair confuses me," I said. "And this dreadful passivity. I keep thinking: 'She is not herself.' She is certainly not the Kate I knew before, but does that mean that she is an impostor? How can I expect her to be the same after all she has been through? And another thing: How could the Hashashin ever hope to find a Vietnamese who looks so much like Kate at such short notice?"

"There are a number of Vietnamese refugees in this country today. It might not be too difficult to find a girl who looked like Kate among the Eurasian orphans."

166

"What are we going to do about it?"

"Nothing, for a while. We'll just have to act as if we believe she is Kate. Then, if she is an impostor, she may get careless and give herself away."

"I don't know if I can do that."

"You'll have to for everybody's sake."

"And Jade? Do we tell her?"

"No. She's had enough. We must spare her as long as there is any chance this girl may turn out to be the real Kate after all."

I pushed away my glass of cognac, unfinished. I had lost my taste for it.

"What about the police? Do we tell them anything?"

"Not until we're sure ourselves. No matter who this girl is, the police will want to prosecute her as a member of a conspiracy to extort money from Adam which ended in his murder."

"Then we should smuggle her into Connecticut so she can surrender to Connecticut State Police," I said. "After all, both crimes were committed in Connecticut."

"And what's your real reason?"

"Captain Carew would be in charge of the investigation in Connecticut. I know and trust him."

"You think the FBI would rather the case was tried here in New York?"

"Digby would play a bigger role then and get a larger share of publicity. He might argue that it's an interstate case because the kidnappers brought their alleged victim across state lines."

Ghislain rose and walked over to the windows. He parted the curtains of one just enough for him to look down into the courtyard.

"Spooks?"

"None in view at the moment, but I think we should get her to Connecticut as soon as possible." He let the curtains fall together again.

"Tonight?"

"Better five o'clock tomorrow morning. Kate must have a few hours sleep."

"Kate?"

Ghislain's smile was twisted. "We'll have to go on calling her Kate and thinking of her as Kate as long as we can. Otherwise, she'll suspect that we suspect her and, once that happens, we may never know who she is. Where's your car, Sam?"

"In Stamford, at a garage."

"Then you'll have to rent a car to drive Jade and Kate to Connecticut. I'll use my own car to pick up my lawyer and I'll leave the house first so, if there's anyone watching, he'll follow my car instead of yours."

"Where do we meet? Carew's office?"

"It would be less conspicuous to meet at your house."

"Is this lawyer a criminal lawyer?"

"No, but he can tell us whom to get. Kate should have the best when she faces Carew."

"And do we tell the lawyers our doubts about Kate's identity?"

"We'll have to eventually." Ghislain's glance lingered on my face. "I wish I could know what you are really thinking."

"I wish I knew myself," I answered him. "But I don't. I can only tell you what I think I'm thinking."

"What's that?"

"If she is the real Kate, it was Adam's death that broke her. I don't know why the Hashashin should want to kill him, but, if they did, I think they are perfectly capable of using his death to destroy her normal personality."

"How can we ever prove any of that?"

"We can't, unless the Hashashin themselves tell the truth, and they won't, because that would incriminate them."

"Then our only hope is a lawyer smart enough to break one of them on the witness stand?" demanded Ghislain.

"Exactly."

"I sometimes wonder if the adversary system is the best way to get at the truth in court. Isn't it just the old mediaeval trial-by-combat with tricks and money taking the place of lance and sword? Is a fight between two men really the best way to get at the truth? It's not the way scientists use."

I finished my cognac after all and rose. "So, for a few days more, Jade will live in a fool's Paradise?"

"That, my friend, is better than no Paradise at all. In effect, it's the only Paradise most of us will ever know."

The door opened. Jade and the girl I still thought of as Kate stood on the threshold. Jade had no doubts. Her face glowed with that radiance that comes from within and one arm was around the girl's shoulders.

This Kate was not the Kate I had known, but wasn't she still Kate? How could she go through such a revolution in experience and not suffer a change in personality?

She was far too thin, but at least she was now cleaner and more relaxed than when I had found her. She still looked like someone who was just waking from a long nightmare, but wasn't that only natural?

Jade had wound a white towel around her head like a turban, hiding the unbecoming, red-dyed hair. Now the grime was washed away from her face I could see a bruise on one smooth, ivory cheek. The dark eyes were feverishly brilliant and all her movements were loose, jerky and uncertain.

This frightened me. I remembered men I had seen in a state of combat fatigue. There had been just this same curious kind of looseness and uncertainty about them, manifest in walk, gesture and expression, all physical signs by which we recognize one another. They had looked quite literally as if they were "coming apart" and this disintegration was often a prelude to violence against themselves or others.

It is as catastrophic to fool with the forces that hold a

169

personality together as it is to fool with the forces that hold the atom together. A normal personality, like normal matter, seems so real, solid and commonplace that we cannot believe it could ever be dissolved, but it can.

Personality and matter are held together by the tremendous force of an invisible power. Once the unity of either is breached, the same power that held them together drives them apart in cataclysmic explosion. You cannot put an atom together again. I, for one, doubt if you can put a personality together again quite as often or as easily as some psychiatrists would like us to believe.

Jade brought her to the cushioned sofa that faced the fire, made her lie on it and drew a light knitted afghan over her knees and feet.

"She doesn't talk much," said Jade. "But I suppose that's to be expected."

I remembered how Zombie had not talked at all.

Kate—what else could I call her?—smiled at me, but it was a groping, insecure smile, no warmth or familiarity in it at all. It was almost as if she had never seen me before tonight.

She clasped her hands in her lap. Surely those were the hands I had always admired, so long, so narrow, so flexible and graceful?

Ghislain spoke quietly. "Has she had anything to eat?"

"A little warm milk," said Jade. "She's more tired than hungry. I think we should get her to bed."

The girl lay there as if she didn't hear the things that were being said about her. Her gaze was fixed on the fire, but she was looking through it, or beyond it, towards something in her own mind only she could see.

Ghislain leaned forward and touched her hand gently to draw her attention. "Kate, do you think you will be able to drive as far as Connecticut tomorrow?"

She didn't answer him. She just looked at her mother. I had never seen anyone quite so utterly passive.

170

Jade said: "Darling, do you think you'll feel up to such a drive? It's about sixty-five miles. It will take around two hours allowing for traffic and so forth."

The soft answer was scarcely audible. The words were spoken without any emotional response at all.

"I suppose so."

If the dead could speak, they would speak that way.

Jade rose. "Come, Kate, dear. I'm going to see you have a good night's rest."

"Good night, Kate." I wanted to kiss her but I didn't dare. Being with her now was like walking on eggs while trying not to break any. I had a feeling that the less I did or said the better. She needed rest even more than love.

I think Ghislain felt something the same way. He didn't even say "good night." He just smiled.

When the door closed, he looked at me.

"Well?"

"She's very like Kate," I answered. "And Jade has no doubts."

"I've told you Jade doesn't want to have doubts."

"Neither do I."

"Are there many changes?"

"Only what you might expect. There were a lot of changes in me when I got out of Vietnam. You get over things physically, but you never get over them mentally."

"Then this girl could be Kate?"

"Oh, yes. I wouldn't question it if you hadn't planted a doubt in my mind."

"Do you think she can stand the trip?"

"Better than she could stand a trial in New York where people are even more hostile to her."

"Wouldn't New York have to extradite her to Connecticut for trial? Both the kidnapping and Adam's murder occurred there."

"You're probably right, but I think it's important that her

first contact with police should be with a man like Carew. A lot depends on preliminary questioning."

"Then we'd better leave as early as possible tomorrow morning. I'll call my lawyer now. Shall I ask him to recommend a psychiatrist as well?"

"Perhaps we need a psychiatrist more than we need a lawyer," I said. "In this case, Kate is both accuser and accused. She is accusing the Hashashin of abducting her and they are accusing her of becoming an accessory after the fact through a voluntary conversion to their cause. Her guilt or innocence will be determined by something that is almost impossible to prove: her state of mind while she was with the Hashashin. They can only exculpate themselves by destroying her and they'll spare no effort to do so."

Ghislain began dialling the telephone.

I rose, but he waved me back to my chair.

"You're staying in our guest room tonight. We should leave for Connecticut as early as we can tomorrow morning."

17

Comparatively few New Yorkers know their city at dawn. At that hour most of the night workers have gone home and the drunks are sleeping it off. Yet dawn is the hour when great cities are at their most appealing. The rest of the time you can't see the city for the people.

I, who had crossed Brooklyn Bridge so many times at sunset, now crossed it for the first time at sunrise. A brilliant red light in the east brought a blush like a faint echo to the Jersey palisades. The old streets around City Hall were as empty as a city of the dead. Lower Broadway looked as forsaken as all Manhattan may look in a thousand years when Macaulay's New Zealander digs into the radioactive rubble and anthropologists hotly deny the crackpot theory that human beings once lived here.

As we approached 23rd Street, I wondered if Kate would show any awareness of what had happened there only last night but she didn't.

She and Jade sat together in the back of the rented car. I could see Kate clearly in the rear-view mirror. Her head rested on Jade's shoulder and her eyes were lost in some dream or memory. Jade had dressed her in inconspicuous gray with a hat to hide her ruined hair and cast a shadow over her face so she would be hard to recognize at a glance.

I forced myself to drive well below the speed limit. If we were picked up for speeding now and Kate was recognized, it would spoil our whole plan for her.

Without people and cars, all the streets looked wider and the vistas longer. Fifty-seventh Street was as deserted as a ballroom when all the guests have gone home.

By the time we picked up the West Side Highway and left the city behind us, the sky was a tender blue and the whole world seemed fresh and new as Eden.

At the Greenwich toll booth we came to the sign that reads: WELCOME TO CONNECTICUT.

Tension flowed out of me. We were home, free and dry. I picked up more speed now and our shadow, long in the light of early morning, ran beside us.

Connecticut had never looked more springlike. The trees along the Merritt Parkway were in full green leaf now and the forsythia was like living sunshine.

I took the Black Rock Turnpike exit instead of Sport Hill Road because I didn't want to pass Adam's house. If this was my Kate in the back seat, I didn't want to remind her of things better forgotten now.

As we pulled into my own driveway, Jade said: "Did you leave anyone in charge?"

"A young man named Neil Ormsby. He knows Kate."

Jade turned to the girl. "Do you remember him?"

"Vaguely. I meet so many people."

It was exactly the sort of thing she would say if she were a changeling and it was exactly the sort of thing that Kate herself might say if Neil had made less impression on her than she had on him.

The gates were standing open as I had usually left them myself. We took the fork in the driveway that led to the gatehouse.

As we walked up the path, a dog began to bark. Kate

174

stopped. A light came into her eyes. "Robbie . . ."

I unlocked the front door. Robbie danced out of the house and ran rings around Kate, barking.

She sat down on the front step and took him in her arms.

Jade looked at me: "There is one person who remembers Kate."

I had not the heart to tell her that Robbie was the world's worst watch dog, that he would welcome anyone who approached him amiably.

I went to the foot of the stairs and called: "Neil?"

But it was the kitchen door that opened.

"Sam! I thought I heard Rob barking but it never occurred to me that it was you."

Neil was in robe and slippers. When he saw Jade, poised in the doorway slender and vivid as a dragonfly, he remembered his tousselled hair and tried to smooth it down with his hands.

"This is Neil Ormsby," I said. "Madame de Boisron, Kate's mother."

Neil's astonishment made him look younger than he actually was. "Is . . . Kate here?"

"Yes." Jade turned in the doorway. "Kate, here is someone who remembers you."

She came forward slowly.

"We used to meet at dances in Fairfield," said Neil. "You probably don't remember me at all."

"Oh, but I do now I see you."

Exactly what she would say if she did not remember him at all. She had always been a polite child.

"You don't know how glad I am to see you free."

Her smile wavered like a smile reflected in moving water. "You don't know how glad I am to be free."

"Have you had breakfast?"

"Thank you, we had breakfast before we left New York," said Jade.

"Coffee, at least?"

"That would be pleasant."

"I usually make instant," Neil was saying. "But there's some sort of drip pot here, if anyone can show me how to use it."

"That's mine," I said. "Lead me to it."

"Either way it won't take a minute," went on Neil. "The water's boiling now."

"And where is the kitchen?" asked Jade.

Robbie was running beside us as we moved into the kitchen. Suddenly he sat down and began to bark again.

"Quiet, pup," said Neil automatically.

But Robbie ran back into the hall, still barking.

It did not sound like a watch dog's bark. It sounded like a friendly, interested bark that seems to say: "Hello, look who's here?" Knowing Robbie, I still think that is the kind of bark it was.

"It must be Ghislain," Jade explained to Neil. "My husband is coming to meet us here with a lawyer and a doctor and—"

We were all in the kitchen when the front door crashed open.

On the threshold stood Al Jebble, holding a businesslike Colt .45. The way he was aiming it at me told me that he knew the most painful, fatal wounds are abdominal wounds.

Kate was the first to move.

She stepped in front of me and hurled the kettle of boiling water at Al.

As the splash scalded his hand, he fired and dropped the gun simultaneously. The bullet went wild, but that was chance. Once she had stepped in front of me, she was the target.

Al turned and ran to an unfamiliar car in the driveway.

By the time I got my rented car turned around, his car was pelting towards Sport Hill Road.

Speed limits no longer existed for him. We went up and down Meeker Hill and skidded around the next curve. I began

176

to worry about the rotary where the Easton-Westport road crosses Sport Hill. At this hour of the morning there would be commuter cars hurrying to Saugatuck station. At this speed Al was not going to be able to stop for any stop signs.

Yet he actually increased his speed as he turned into Sport Hill Road.

That was his mistake. The curve there is tighter than it looks. He couldn't slow down once he was into the curve. His car left the road and plowed through some bushes and slammed into the broad trunk of an old oak tree.

I left my car and ran to him.

The steering wheel had crushed and pierced his chest but he was still alive and conscious. I remembered how long it had taken to kill Rasputin.

"I'll get an ambulance," I said.

He shook his head. "Don't bother. This is it. But there's one thing I must tell you: I did not kill Adam Endicott. Neither did Moon Mother or Fox Maiden. I was the man who fired at you so Kate Endicott could be kidnapped but I did not kill her father. He was alive when he gave us the ransom money. We didn't know he was dead until we saw it in the papers . . ."

"Did the Old Man of the Mountain kill him?"

Incredibly he began to laugh. There were pink bubbles of bloody saliva on his lips, but he was still laughing.

"I fooled you. On that first tape I told you my name was Hassan-ben-Sabah, Sheikh al Jebal, the same as the founder of the old Hashashin. The Agency people and Moon Mother never could say it right. They said Al Jebble, but they meant al Jebal. Can't you guess what Sheikh al Jebal means? Old Man of the Mountain."

"So you were the Old Man of the Mountain yourself?"

"Yes, but nobody knew. Then, when I had to say 'no' to my people, I didn't have to take the blame. I could say I was just taking orders from him . . ."

He was gasping now but there was something he had to say.

"That's the sort of trick the first al Jebal used to play on his boys . . . when they first joined up, he told'em there was a Great Secret . . . the Secret of the Universe. . . . But he wouldn't tell'em what it was. . . . Not 'till they'd worked their way through five degrees of initiation . . . Lasik or Brethren . . . Fedavee or Executioners . . . Rafeek or Fellows . . . Dais or Nuncios . . . Dai-il-Kebeer or Grand Recruiters. . . . That took twenty years . . . or more . . . but only those who could stand the racket were worthy of the Great Secret of the Universe in the end. . . . And what was it? That closely guarded secret? Can't you guess?"

"No, but who—"

He was trying to laugh. "The Great Secret was . . . that there was no secret! . . . All the Hashashin wanted was money . . . like all the rest of us . . . but you had to work through five degrees before they told you. . . . And maybe that's still the Great Secret of the Universe . . . that there is none. . . ."

"But who did kill Adam Endicott?"

"It was . . ."

His jaw sagged. His eyes glazed.

Another car came along a moment later, so I could ask the driver to call Captain Carew while I stayed with the body.

When Carew and I got to the gatehouse there were several other people on the terrace besides Kate and Jade and Neil. Ghislain had arrived with two strangers, the lawyer and the psychiatrist. Isolda had come with Clara and Joey.

They all looked as ill-assorted and uneasy with each other as people thrown together by a shipwreck or a house on fire.

It was on Kate that Carew's attention focused.

"Is that really Kate Endicott?" he asked me.

"That is really Kate Endicott."

"You're sure?"

"I'm absolutely sure now."

Isolda was not happy to see me after our last meeting. Joey didn't know what to say to Kate after the things he had written about her in newspapers and magazines when apparently he had assumed she was dead and so would never be able to dispute anything he wrote. Even Clara was subdued and uncertain of herself now.

She was speaking to Neil when I reached the terrace.

"I had no idea you would be here."

"Didn't you? I've been keeping an eye on things here for Sam while he was away. Excuse me a moment, I haven't really had a chance to talk to Kate yet."

Clara watched him cross the terrace to Kate's side, then became aware of me watching her.

Immediately she began to explain her presence.

"We were in Captain Carew's office when Kate's stepfather came in to tell him Kate was here. Mother insisted that she and Joey and I should come back here to see Kate, but I think it was a mistake. I don't believe Kate wants to see us now. I suppose it's because of all those things Joey wrote about her. She never was in love with him, you know. I don't suppose she's ever been in love with anybody."

"Don't you?"

"Have you ever seen her really warm up to a boy?"

I couldn't resist that one. "Perhaps she'd rather have a man."

"You mean an old man?"

Fortunately I didn't have to answer that because Carew was speaking to all of us now.

"Sheikh al Jebal, or Al Jebble as many people called him, the leader of the Hashashin, has just died in a car accident. He insisted that neither he nor the other kidnappers killed Adam Endicott and he claimed that he had no idea who did. Do any of you know anything that might throw further light on Adam Endicott's death?"

179

"I've told you everything I know," I said. "But I have some guesses that I haven't told anybody."

"Let's hear them."

"Al Jebble did not say that the kidnappers did not kill Endicott. Al Jebble said that he and Moon Mother and Fox Maiden did not kill Endicott. Why did he name those three individuals instead of just saying the 'kidnappers'? Could it be that those three were not the only people involved in the kidnapping?

"I was there the night it happened. There was a tall, thin woman, wearing a long dress and a stocking mask. There was a tall, robust man in jeans, masked the same way. The man was Al Jebble. He admitted that, but who was the woman?

"Moon Mother was tall, but she was large, heroic, an Amazon. Fox Maiden was short, wizened, stringy. Who was that tall woman and how did she and Al Jebble know just when Kate would be in the kitchen that night?

"I've always felt the kidnappers knew more about the plan of the house and the schedule of the household than outsiders like the Hashashin could possibly have known unless they had an accomplice inside. It was an amateur crime, but it was not a crime of gypsies like the Hashashin. They were being used all along by someone with both feet on the ground.

"It was the man who actually spoke to Kate that night, not the woman. Did she keep quiet because she was afraid her voice might be recognized?"

Isolda broke the silence and her voice was now like steel.

"I may be tall, but I was in the kitchen with you, Sam, when this happened."

"Yes, but what about your daughter, Clara, who is so tall she looks elongated like a reflection in a trick mirror? Was she in New York that night as she was supposed to be? And what about her friend, Joey, who got us all into the kitchen at exactly the right moment for the kidnapping? I think you suspect your daughter already. I think that is why you came to see me in New York. You wanted to find out how much I knew or guessed."

Kate was looking at Clara with horror.

"This is ridiculous!" Clara's voice sounded like her mother's now. "Kate was my friend, my best friend."

"There is one thing that can always break up a friendship," I said. "Its name is jealousy and one of the oldest songs in the world tells us that 'it is cruel as the grave: the coals thereof are coals of fire, which hath a most vehement flame.'

"You were the tall woman in the stocking mask who never spoke, but how could Kate possibly suspect her best friend, Clara?

"She never saw you with the Hashashin except that one time during the kidnapping when you were masked and silent. She was locked in the trunk of the kidnapping car immediately and when she was taken out at the old Delano place, you had gone.

"Did you import the Hashashin from New York and tell them they could camp out at the Delano place? And promise them ransom money from Adam if they kidnapped Kate? Did you love someone who loved Kate more than he loved you? Someone like Neil perhaps? Moon Mother and Fox Maiden were the only women whose voices were on the tapes, but you were the moving spirit of the whole thing, you and Joey.

"You hated Kate because she was not the kind of refugee you could patronize. If she had been less pretty and less fortunate, if she had been old and sick and poor, she would not have provoked quite the same fervor of patriotism in you and Joey."

"She told me it was a joke!" shouted Joey. "Just a fun thing, a practical joke, to put a scare into Kate and take her down a peg because Neil had always been Clara's until Kate came along. I understood how Clara felt because Kate brushed me off the way Neil brushed off Clara.

"There were a lot of people who didn't like Kate at school,

181

especially girls. Who was Kate anyway? An enemy from a country that had been fighting us for years."

"Shut up, Joey!" said Clara through her clenched teeth. "So we played a joke on Kate. So what? That doesn't prove Joey or I shot Adam Endicott."

Joey gasped. "Clara, don't talk about shooting. Are you suggesting I did it? You know I didn't shoot him."

"Are you suggesting I did?"

"I'm remembering things. Later, that night, you gave me the ransom money and told me to hide it at my house until the Hashashin went back to New York. You said no one would look for it at my house because I wasn't under suspicion. So I did what you said, but, Clara, where were you while I was doing that?"

"Kindly hold your tongue, Joey, will you?"

"I left you alone with Endicott. Did he recognize you then? He might have. He'd known you for years. And, if he did, you'd have to kill him, wouldn't you? And you could have, because you had Al's gun. He and Moon Mother and Zombie had all gone on to the Delano place, and Kate was still in the trunk of the car, so it had to be you . . ."

As I write these last lines I am sitting in the garden of a villa at Cap d'Antibes, which belongs to Ghislain's grandmother. Kate has just come in from a swim. Her hair is black again. Her ivory skin is golden from the sun. No one can look at her now and believe that she was so close to death only a few months ago.

I have been doing more research on the Hashashin.

I came across one line that chills me: "There are those who say that, even today, a few descendants of the ancient Hashashin can still be found practicing their lethal arts secretly in the Ansariyeh mountains of Syria."